The Wife Of A Kingpin 2
Malik & Micah's Story

By: Twyla T. & Patrice Balark

Copyright

Publishers Note

Published by Cole Hart Presents

This is a work of fiction. Names, characters, places, and events are strictly the product of the author or used fictitiously. Any similarities between actual persons, living or dead, events, settings, or locations are entirely coincidental.

Text TwylaT to 21000 to stay up to date on new releases, plus get information on contests, sneak peeks, and more!!!!

Dedication

This book is dedicated to the awesome readers that are in Cole Hart Signature Readers Club. Because of the platform Cole has provided for all of his authors, we have the chance to showcase our talents with the hopes that we can gain loyal readers. We've watched each of you give us chances, and if you're reading this right now... you've done it again!! We thank you all sooo much!!

Twyla & Patrice

Twyla T's Acknowledgments

As always, I must first acknowledge and thank God because without him, none of this would be possible. Next, I have to thank Patrice for taking me up on my offer to do this collaboration. It has been so much fun. I hope that everyone enjoys it as much as we enjoyed writing it. Last but certainly not least, shout out to everyone who is a part of Twyla T's Reading Group. You all took a chance on me and have really been holding me down. I can't thank y'all enough!!

When you are done, please leave a review on Amazon, Good Reads, and/or any of my social media pages so that I can read your feedback and make adjustments. My Facebook, Instagram, and Twitter handles are all @authortwylat

You may also email me at authortwylat@gmail.com and check out my website authortwylat.com

Search Twyla T's Reading Group on Facebook if you love my work and become a

supporter! We love to kick back and have fun in there, and there also random giveaways!

Other great reads by Author Twyla T:

We Both Can't Be Bae 1-3

I'll Never Love A Dope Boy Again 1 & 2

My Shawty 1-3 (An Original Love Story)

Pretty Lips That Thugs Love 1-4

Patrice Balark's Acknowledgments

Fuck Mobb Deep, fuck Biggie, fuck Bad Boy as a staff, record label and as a motherfucking crew!

And if you want to be down with Bad Boy, then fuck you too!

Chino XL: fuck you too!

Great Reads by Patrice Balark:

High Maintenance 1-4

Lovin' A Chi Town Kingpin 1-2

Black Tonya 1-2

Last time in The Wife of a Kingpin: Malik & Micah's Story...

Things finally seemed to be looking up for Tasha, and she couldn't be happier. A couple of weeks had passed since her and Micah's last spat, and they were finally back on speaking terms. After thinking long and hard about their friendship, Tasha decided that she really wanted it back and was going to end her bullshit behaviors once and for all. She was still a bit salty about the friendship that Micah had built with Candy, but told herself that as long as it wasn't thrown in her face, everything was good.

Tasha headed towards The Factory listening to Bad and Boujee by Migos while smoking some backwood and getting in her zone. It was Saturday night and there was money to be made. Just the thought of money being thrown at her, made her pussy wet. Tasha wanted to beat her own ass for not taking the dancing route sooner than she did. She was a beast with it and loved it. Tasha turned into the parking lot and it was already packed, just as she expected. After she parked, Tasha grabbed her bag and went inside.

"What up sexy?" the security guard spoke and let her in.

"Nothin' much big daddy... just ready to make this money baby," Tasha responded.

As she headed towards her locker, she heard a couple of whistles, along with lips smacking and mumbling from some nearby women. Tasha looked at a couple of them, cocked her head to the side, and then smiled and continued on her way. She was used to attention and she loved it all, both positive and negative. As long as a bitch didn't approach her, she was Gucci. Money and dick were the top two things on her mind, not fighting hoes and taking a chance on fucking up her skin.

Twenty minutes later, Tasha sauntered on stage to do her set. She looked over the crowd and smiled because all her eyes saw was money, money, and more money. When the music cued, she started doing her thang to Bounce It by Juicy J.

Yeah... yeah

We gon' stay trippy for life man

Yeah, I'm bout to take your girl…

Bounce it, bounce it

I'm about to throw a couple thousand

Bounce it, bounce it

I'm about to throw a couple thousand

Ones, fives, tens, twenties

Work your way to the big face hundreds, just bounce

Bounce it, bounce it

I'm about to throw a couple thousand…

Tasha chose that particular song because she wanted the men to get loose and come up off the dough that was in their pockets. The shit worked because by the time the song ended, the stage was full of so much money. When she saw that bills were still being thrown, she gave the DJ the signal to run it back one time. He did just what she asked, and Tasha popped her pussy and never missed a beat. By the time the song was done for the second time, Tasha had money on every part of her body that could hold it, and the stage was still covered.

As she made her exit from the stage, she locked eyes with a man that she had never seen before. Tasha bypassed her regular customers and sashayed up to the fresh meat. There was some type of mystery feel to him as she approached him, but that didn't stop Tasha. She was always up for a challenge.

"You see something you like?" Tasha whispered into his ear once she made it close enough to lean up.

"Meet me in one of the private rooms after you freshen up," the man said in a deep voice that sounded like Barry White. He never cracked a smile, in fact, his face seemed to hold a permanent grimace, but Tasha paid it no mind.

"See you soon!" she exclaimed and sauntered off.

Almost thirty minutes later, Tasha was fresh and ready to face off with the mystery man. She stashed her belongings in her locker, and then headed towards the back. For some strange reason, the security guy who was normally on the post to guard the rooms was gone, but Tasha shrugged it off and went about her way. She had no idea which rooms were already occupied, but when she twisted the first doorknob, it opened so Tasha knew that it was vacant.

Just as she suspected, the man was sitting on the recliner with the same expression on his face. Tasha felt like it was about to take some of her magic head to get him to loosen up, and she was definitely up for the challenge. With no words spoken, she walked over to him and immediately fell to her knees. Tasha unzipped his pants, released his dick and teased it with the tip of her tongue. It wasn't the length and width that she liked, but it was doable, so she went to work on it.

She felt the man moan a little and then he began to move. Just when she thought that he was finally getting into it, Tasha heard a click and looked up and her eyes met the barrel of a silver gun. When she tried to move, he grabbed her neck.

"Don't fuckin move or I'll be forced to blow your brains out," the man harshly spoke.

"Whaa... what... what do you want?" Tasha stuttered.

"You have connections that I need. You run in plenty of circles. I been watching you. You're gonna bring me all of the information I need, and you're gonna do it smartly. I'm gonna give you this piece of paper with my info, and you are to report to me daily. This ain't a fuckin joke either," the man stated.

"Who... who do I have to get information on?" Tasha asked with tears streaming down her face.

"Your best friend, her man, and his partner... now clean yourself up and don't fuck with me either. I know everything I need to know about you... including your ties with Mo. So both of y'all can get the job done," the man said and got up and left after he fixed his pants.

Tasha cried her eyes out. Just when her and Micah had gotten back on track, she was forced to do more grimy shit.

"Fuck!" Tasha spat.

***

A week had passed since the incident at the mall between Candy and Mona. Mona was mad for about a day, while Candy never removed Goo from her block list. He even stopped by her condo two days ago, and she still didn't answer the door for him. Goo wasn't sure what exactly was going on with her, but it was starting to piss him off. He even reached out to Micah via text message to check on Candy, and Micah responded dry as fuck by just stating that she was cool. Having women problems was new to him. Although he always had a gang of bitches on his team, he only loved Mona and knew at the end of the day, that's where he would end up but Candy changed the game when she came into his life.

"Goo baby, please be careful with my eggs; you break them, I will kill you." Mona threatened as they walked in the house with bags full of groceries they got from Walmart and Food 4 Less.

Mona told Goo that she had a special night planned for them. She advised him that she was going to start things off by making his favorite, seafood. They went to two stores and gathered all the things they needed for the meal: lobster tails, shrimps, scallops, baked potatoes and garlic bread. After he helped Mona take the things out of the bags, Goo headed upstairs to shower. The entire time in the shower, he couldn't stop thinking about Candy. Yeah, he was satisfied with Mona, but he was happy with Candy and was a totally different man. He thought about sitting the two of them down and explaining how he wanted things to play out. Goo wanted to come clean with Candy and let her know all about his dealings in the street, but just as quick as that thought entered his mind, it left.

Goo always seemed to forget that she was still "Attorney Candice Williams" and knew how bitter women could be. The last thing he needed was a scorned, broken-hearted-baby momma of a lawyer coming after him. Flashbacks of the times they spent together invaded his thoughts next. Thinking about the way he would bend her over the balcony in her condo caused his dick to stand at full attention. The way her thick frame looked on top of him while she rode his dick backwards caused Goo to start stroking his dick. Mona had a good head on her shoulders, but Candy was a scholar. Her head game drove Goo insane, she was perfect for him in so many ways.

"Did you drown?" Mona's voice rang from the other side of the door.

"Nah, here I come," he replied and rinsed the remaining soap off his body and hopped out the shower.

Goo dried off before entering the connecting bedroom that he shared with his wife. Mona was laid across the bed, scrolling through her phone.

"How you cooking from a distance?" he asked, searching through the top drawer for a pair of underwear.

"I'm almost done, you been in the shower since forever, the potatoes are in the oven," Mona looked up from the phone and informed him.

"Cool because I'm hungry than a muthafucker," Goo replied, dropping his towel to the ground.

"Looks like somebody else is hungry too," she said seductively while eyeing his erected penis.

Goo thought that he pushed the thoughts of Candy to the back of his mind but apparently, he didn't do a good job at it because his dick was as hard as it's ever been.

"Yeah, bend over so I can handle that," Goo instructed as he walked over to the bed where Mona was still laying.

Mona quickly jumped up and removed the leggings she was wearing and tossed them to the side. She then followed Goo's instructions and bent over, putting her perfectly round ass high in the air. Goo held his dick in his hands and guided his way inside of her warm, yet soaking wet pussy. Mona formed the perfect arch and allowed Goo to go to work. He rammed his nine inches in and out of her while she moaned loudly with pleasure.

"I love this dick Rico. Oh my God!" she screamed but instead of responding, Goo closed his eyes and imagined it was Candy he was fucking instead of Mona.

Goo felt himself reaching his peak just when his iPhone started to ring. He ignored the call because at that moment busting a nut was more important. Whoever it was, he was going to call them back.

Ring. Ring. Ring.

The caller hung up and called right back and just like the previous time, he ignored it again.

"Damn Cand….Mona, I'm finna nut," Goo felt himself almost slip up and call Mona Candy's name.

He paused in mid stroke just to see if she heard him but the way she was screaming out, he knew that she hadn't.

Ring. Ring. Ring.

The sound alerting him that he had a FaceTime call, was now buzzing through the room. Goo looked to the right of him where his phone was lying face up on the nightstand and noticed it was Micah, who was Facetiming him. It was unlikely for her to text him or even call, so he knew something had to be wrong if she was blowing his phone up. The first thing that came to his mind was something had happened to Malik so without thinking twice, he slid the bar on the phone, accepting the call.

"What's wrong?" He questioned, as soon as the call connected.

"It's Candy, she was just rushed to the hospital," Micah replied urgently.

"She in labor?" Goo bubbled excitedly, pulling his now softened dick out of Mona.

"Yeah Goo but I don't think she's good. She was bleeding really bad. The baby might be in danger." she replied.

"WHAT THE FUCK? WHAT HOSPITAL SHE IS AT?" Goo yelled while throwing on his drawers and some Nike sweatpants.

"Northwestern. I'll meet you up there as soon as I drop something off to Malik," she said before ending the call.

Goo threw a white t-shirt on with a Nike hoodie to match, a pair of all-white Air Force Ones, then grabbed his wallet off the dresser along with the keys to his Jaguar and headed out the door.

"I FUCKIN' HATE YOU RICO! YOU REALLY FINNA LEAVE ME?" Mona yelled out to him, her voice filled with hurt.

Goo stopped at the stairs and turned around, heading back to the bedroom, where he stood in the doorway watching his wife break down.

"I'm sorry baby but I gotta go. I know you heard Micah, Candy's at the hospital," Goo reminded her.

"Do I look like I give a fuck about what that bitch Micah said, and furthermore, do I look like I give a fuck about yo mistress being in labor? I am your wife Rico. I set this night up for you. I told you I have a surprise for you and this is the thanks I get? You dropping everything and leaving me because she needs you?" she sobbed.

Goo knew the way he just went about things was wrong and hurtful, but he couldn't help it. Candy and his son was more important than Mona at this very moment. This was just something that Mona had to grow to understand.

"Look, I'll call you from the hospital but I gotta go," he said walking away again.

"I HATE YOU. I HOPE HER AND THAT BABY DIE!" Mona screamed at the top of her lungs.

The words that Mona just let escape her mouth pissed him off, but that's something he would have to address later and that's something he wouldn't forget to do. Regardless of how mad she was, saying shit like that about somebody's kid could get you killed.

Goo drove the shoulder of the expressway the entire ride downtown to Northwestern Hospital. He parked right in front, not worrying about getting a ticket or getting his shit towed. He had wasted enough time away from Candy during her pregnancy, and it was time for him to be present and active, regardless of how anybody felt.

"Ummmm… Candance Williams?" he said to the receptionist at the front desk.

After keying a few things into the system, she handed him a visitor pass and told him to take the elevator up to the seventh floor where labor and delivery was located. Once Goo got off at the appointed floor, he spoke to the nurses on duty at the nurse's station located there before they directed him to the room Candy was in. Without knocking, Goo busted through the doors where he found Candy laying in the hospital bed plugged up to a bunch of machines.

"I'll be in the waiting room if you need me," a woman whom Goo never met before said, getting out of her seat and exiting the room.

"Are you ok? Is the baby ok?" He asked, standing on the side of her bed.

"Yeah I think so. I'm waiting on the nurses to come back now," Candy softly whispered.

"Well what happened?" Goo asked, tired of receiving second-hand knowledge of the happenings with Candy and their baby.

"I was at home and felt a gush of liquor running down my legs. I thought my water broke but when I looked down, my pants were covered in blood," she recanted.

"Damn, I'm so sorry Candy. I should have been there, it's all my fault," Goo apologized, grabbing her hand.

Just as Candy was getting ready to speak, a bubbly nurse entered the room.

"Hello, you must be dad?" She said, extending her arm for a handshake.

Goo nodded his head up and down, while shaking her hand.

"Mommy gave us a pretty good scare here, but I'm happy to report that not only is mommy going to be ok, but the baby is doing great. We ran a few tests to see what caused the bleeding and your system tested positive for oxytocin, which is weird because that medicine is given to you when we are inducing labor. Do you have any idea how that got into your system?" The nurse asked.

"Well I'm not sure. I went to my doctor's appointment as normal. They did the same routine shit and then gave me a shot," she explained.

"A shot? Who gave you a shot?" The nurse quizzed.

"The Medical Assistant did. I asked her about it and she said it's something that they give patients when they are close to delivery," Candy responded.

"Do you remember the Medical Assistant's name?" The nurse drilled.

"She was new. I've never seen her before, but I believe it was Tammy Simpson. Yeah that's her name, I remember asking her twice. Is something wrong?" A worried Candy inquired.

"Yeah there is, that medicine that she gave you could have killed you and the baby. I'll be back," the nurse rushed off.

Goo stood to Candy's side shocked and in total disbelief. He had heard the name Tammy Simpson before because that was the name of Mona's favorite cousin.

"Baby, how did this nurse look?' Goo asked.

"She was light-skinned, had real short hair and freckles all over her face," Candy recollected.

Goo pulled out his phone to text Mona. That was definitely her ghetto ass cousin. Goo stille wondered how a bitch like her made it through school and got a certificate to work in the medical field. He also knew that it wasn't a coincidence that Candy and the baby almost died after being seen by one of Mona's family members. He just couldn't believe the measures she would go to get rid of the two people he adored the most.

"Is everything ok?" Candy asked, noticing the grim look on Goo's face.

"Yeah I'm good," he lied, bending down placing a soft kiss on her forehead before putting his phone away.

He would handle Mona's ass after he left the hospital, texting her would give her time to think of a lie. Besides, he needed to see her facial expression when she found out he knew what was going on.

"Ok momma, you ready, it's time to check you?" The same nurse returned to the room and announced.

"Bout as ready as I'll ever be," Candy let out a nervous giggle.

Goo looked down at her and smiled. He was beyond happy at this very moment. After all the bullshit him and Candy been through, he was present for the most important part of it all, seeing his only son being brought into this cruel world.

"Ok daddy, we going to prep you next," the nurse informed Goo, while handing him a bag for his belongings.

Goo started by taking off his Rolex and then next he removed his hoodie, causing his phone to fall out of the pocket, hitting the floor. Goo said a silent prayer before picking it up and turning it over. This was his third phone this month, he seemed to shatter the screen whenever he dropped it. Goo let out a sigh of relief, when he noticed that the screen was still intact and also noticed he had received a text message from Mona. Goo debated on whether or not he should even read it because he was ready to kill her for almost killing his son and his son's mother. But the curiosity was killing him so he used his thumb to unlock the phone, prompting the unread message to appear across his screen.

Wifey: I'm tired of you hurting me, this night was supposed to be special for US not you and that bitch but I guess life has a way of throwing curve balls…. Anyway….. Congratulations on your "bundle of joy" I won't be here with champagne and balloons when you get home, I'm done….. I'm leaving you… me and the baby….

Before Mona's words could register with Goo, a text message came through that confirmed it all. Mona sent a picture of a positive pregnancy text, with a note attached

Wifey: Congratulations again, now you are a daddy of TWO!!!

***

The semester was finally over, and Micah was beyond elated. She left U of I burning rubber and headed to the funeral home. It had been a minute since she dropped by, so Micah felt like it was a good time to do so since she had a little extra time on her hands. If Micah would have had it her way, the family business wouldn't be a funeral home, but it was what it was. She hoped that Mesha hadn't eaten yet, so they could go and grab some lunch. The traffic wasn't too heavy, so Micah made it to her destination in less than twenty minutes. She parked in the back and made her way in with her key.

"You have to wait until after hours before you bring any more bodies," Micah heard her dad whisper and say. He must have felt her presence because he turned around and jumped.

"Hey baby girl!" he nervously spoke.

"Hey dad... where's Mesh?" she asked.

"She went out to lunch, but she might be back... go to the front and see," her dad told her.

"I should have called first," Micah mumbled and walked off.

She looked back at her dad and wondered what in the hell was going on. Micah had no idea why he would tell someone to wait and bring bodies after hours. Her dad had been acting strange a lot lately, and it made her think about all of the arguments he had been having with her mom lately. When she made it to the front, she saw that Mesha was indeed gone, but Micah didn't turn around to leave. Instead, she walked to the file cabinet in the next room to snoop around. One would think that everything about the money would be kept in the secretary's office, but it was never set up like that. It had been a long time since she had helped out with the books, but she would definitely know if something was off if she had a few minutes to observe.

Micah hurried over and popped open the second drawer, but to her surprise, things had been rearranged and the books weren't in that drawer. She opened the third one and came up empty handed again. It wasn't until she made it to the very last drawer that Micah found what she was looking for.

"What in the fuck? How?" Micah quizzed as she shuffled through the pages. She couldn't believe what she saw. There had to be some type of mistake because there was no way the funeral home was in the negative by that amount a little over a year ago, but now it was way above its budget. When Micah heard the front door open, she quickly put the books back, closed the drawer and eased back into Mesha's office.

"Hey sis... what you doing here?" Micah heard Mesha ask.

"Hey Mesh... I thought I was gon' catch you before lunch, but I see I didn't and you had other plans anyway," Micah remarked as she locked eyes with Frank, her sister's ex.

"Hey Micah," Frank spoke.

"Frank," Micah dryly replied.

"I'll holla at ya later sis... gonna go grab me something to eat," Micah said and walked out without bothering to address Frank any further.

Micah made her way towards the back so that she could exit the same way that she entered. Before she reached the door, she heard some commotion outside, but that didn't stop her from proceeding forward. When she reached the door, she heard her dad loud and clear telling someone that he specifically told them to wait. In return, someone yelled that they couldn't wait so he better make it happen. Micah opened the door and she couldn't believe her eyes. Lying on the ground were two lifeless bloody bodies. It seems as if she stared at them for an eternity. When she looked back up, she saw a black van as it sped off, and her dad standing there with his hands on his head.

"Go ahead and leave Micah," her dad firmly spoke.

She didn't bother to reply, she just left. Shit at the funeral home was crazier than ever, and Micah began to see that her dad wasn't who he said he was. Just a few months back, neither was she, but thanks to Malik, she was out of the game and only focusing on school. Micah's phone rang a few minutes later, and she smiled when she saw that it was Malik.

"Hey babe," she cooed into the phone.

"What's up baby... what you doin'?" Malik inquired.

"Just left the funeral home and Oh myyy gawwddd... the craziest shit happened," Micah exclaimed.

"Damn… you gon' have to tell me 'bout it later. I need you to do me a favor babe," Malik reasoned with her.

"Sure… what you need?" she asked.

"I need you to go by my office… the very first one I took you to and get that black bag that's on the top shelf in the safe. I'll text you the combination when we hang up. Bring it to the club… and we need to talk about something very important baby," Malik pleaded with her.

She told him okay and hung up, and then headed that way. Micah reminisced back to the first time Malik took her to that particular warehouse. It was his way of seeing if he could trust her, but deep down to her, it made her trust him right away. Malik had shown her so much since then, Micah was still in awe. The trip to Punta Cana was the first one that they took, but it certainly wasn't the last. Malik had taken her on a couple of other quick trips down to Miami and Mexico. They were for business, but he promised that they would get away again very soon.

Micah looked down at her phone after she parked, and she saw the text from Malik letting her know where to get the key from and the combination as promised. She never would have thought to look in a paper bag in the fucking garbage can for a key. Micah smiled because her baby was a true boss and thought of shit that the average mind would never even consider. Just as Micah unlocked the door, her phone chimed with a text.

Candy: I'm in labor because I was bleeding kinda bad, but don't panic… I'm only at like 4 centimeters so there's still a lot of time left.

Micah: What the hell? I'll be on my way as soon as I drop this package off to Malik

Candy: Okay… thank you Micah!

Micah: Girl stop. See you soon!

Micah was thrown off by Candy's text because she still had about five weeks to go. For her to say not to worry, meant to worry in Micah's eyes. She had grown to learn that Candy always tried to keep cool, calm, and collected demeanor, no matter what was going on.

"I bet she didn't even tell Goo... let me call his ass," Micah mumbled to herself.

She called him three times, but he never answered, so Micah sent him a text.

Micah: Your son is on the way!

"Fuck that... let me FaceTime this nigga," Micah mumbled.

When the call connected, Micah informed Goo on what was going on as best as she could. She thought about how it was a shame that he didn't even know which hospital his son was being born at.

After she hung up with Goo, Micah hurried inside so that she could take care of the business for Malik and then get to the hospital to be there for Candy. It was no guarantee that Goo was going to show up, but even if he did, Micah still wanted to be there for her newfound friend. So many people always screamed "no new friends" but she was thankful that Candy was placed in her path. They clicked instantly and Micah had grown to love and admire her.

When she opened the safe, she saw the bag Malik told her to get, so she grabbed it. Just when she was about to close the safe back, a phone caught her eye.

"Is this nigga hiding phones to call bitches now?" Micah mumbled to herself.

She reached down and grabbed the phone, but then she put it back down. Her mind bounced back and forth about trust, but the female in her won. She tapped one of the keys so that she could get a glance at the screensaver, but apparently the phone was powered off or the battery was dead. Curiosity got the best of Micah, and she found herself powering the phone on. When the Sprint icon popped up, she confirmed that the phone was just powered off. Once a picture on the home screen appeared, Micah's heart dropped.

"What the fuck?" she asked herself as tears began to form in her eyes.

Micah rushed out of the warehouse at lightning speed. Although she was pissed the fuck off, she still locked up. Micah sped to the club with blurry eyes and a heart full of rage.

"How could you Malik? How could you do this? Whhhyyy??" she screamed and banged on the steering wheel repeatedly.

Micah made it to the club in record time and double parked upon her arrival. She grabbed the phone that she had thrown onto the passenger seat, popped her glove compartment and retrieved her nine, and exited her car. The bag that Malik asked for was still on the seat, and Micah didn't give a fuck about taking it inside. She entered the club and headed straight upstairs. Her tears flowed nonstop, and she was hurt beyond repair, but Micah willed herself to go forward. She needed answers, and if she didn't get the truth, she was going to have to kill the man that she had fallen in love with.

After she wiped her face off, Micah walked into Malik's office with her gun already drawn. She knew that she had caught him off guard, because his hands went straight into the air.

"What the fu…" he started to ask, but Micah intervened.

"I asked you if you knew my brother… and you told me no. How the fuck did you get his phone?" Micah spat as she walked closer and held up Mark's phone that had a picture of him, her, and Mesha as the screen.

The look on Malik's face was one of guilt, so Micah stepped forward and clicked the safety off.

Turn the page to see what's next ☺

Chapter 1

"Micah… baby, let me explain this shit to you!" Malik reasoned with her.

"I asked you… I asked you if you knew my brother, and you looked me in my eyes and told me no Malik. YOU SAID NO!!" Micah fumed as she stepped closer to the man that she had fallen in love with.

Tears streamed down her face as her pointer finger pulsated on the trigger. Visions of Mark clouded her mind. She didn't know how she could have fallen in love with the man who she now felt like took her one and only brother away from her. The words that Mo spoke to Micah registered into her head. Micah beat herself up for not doing any research of Malik on her own. Truth be told, he "dickmatized" Micah and clouded her vision.

"I told you we had something to talk about… put the damn gun down so we can address the situation," Malik said with a hint of anger laced in his voice.

"You don't have the right to be upset, Malik!" Micah spat as she used her left hand to wipe her tears away.

"You got a fuckin' gun pulled on me and you think I ain't gon' be upset… the fuck?" Malik countered and stepped towards Micah.

POP!!

Micah fired her gun and stared down at Malik when he ducked.

"Be fuckin' still or the next one WILL hit you," Micah stated through gritted teeth.

She watched Malik as he stood back up with both hands raised in the air. Micah didn't want to kill Malik, but she would be going against everything she stood for. She needed to hear him say that he killed her brother before she pulled the trigger.

"Why did you lie to me Malik? Did you kill Mark?" Micah inquired with a pleading sadness in her voice.

"Listen babe… I didn't kill Mark. It's a lot of shit that you don't know. I told you we needed to talk and that's what it's about. Your brother," Malik told her after he took a few deep breaths.

Micah stared at him. She wanted to believe the words that he spoke, but the truth of the matter was, she was conflicted. Since he lied to her the first time, Micah didn't know if she could trust him. Was he only telling her that he didn't kill Mark because she had a gun pulled on him? If Malik didn't kill Mark, did he know who did?" Micah thought back to the day that she heard the devastating news.

It was the spring semester of Micah's junior year in high school. When she woke up that Friday morning, thoughts of skipping evaded her mind, but Micah thought about a Chemistry test she had and knew that she needed to go take it.

"One year and a few months left at Lane Tech and I'm outta there," Micah mumbled as she drug herself out of bed. She hated that school and always wanted to go to Westinghouse, but her mom wasn't having that shit. After Mark got into a fight his freshman year, she had him and Mesha transferred and Micah never even got a chance to go. She was ready to graduate high school since her siblings were out of there. At some point, she didn't know what her rush was, but when she thought about freedom, reality kicked in.

After she brushed her teeth, showered, and threw on a pair of red chucks, some jeans, and a tee shirt, Micah made her way downstairs to the dining room where she found Mark sitting at the table eating the pancakes and sausage their mom hadn't been too long cooked for them. She knew that Mesha was probably already gone to the funeral home for the day as well as her dad.

"Why you dragging today? Didn't you say you had a test in Chem?" Mark asked her.

"Yeah… I'm tired as hell though and just wanted to stay in bed," Micah replied.

"Mommy in the kitchen girl," Mark whispered to her.

"Oh... I thought she was back upstairs," Micah said and went into the kitchen and practically bumped into her mom.

"No, I'm still here and watch your mouth. That's so unlady like to be using profanity," Mrs. Sanders stated.

"Good morning, mom," Micah said and ignored her mother's comment. It was crazy to her how Mark could say and do whatever, but when it came down to her, she always got in trouble.

"You dropping me off at school?" Micah asked her brother as she sat down at the table after fixing her plate.

"Fa sho... picking you up too. Today gon' be an easy day. I gotta help one of my partners setup for a basketball tournament, but that ain't gon' take too long," Mark responded.

"Hurry up... I'll be in the car. Gotta handle some shit right quick," Mark told his sister while texting on his phone and heading to the front door.

Micah finished her breakfast and took her plate back in the kitchen and threw it in the sink. A few moments later, she grabbed her backpack and headed out the door. Patience was something Mark didn't have a lot of, so she knew that time was of the essence. Micah made it outside and hopped into her brother's charcoal gray Infiniti. She could tell that he was having an intense phone conversation by the lines that were displayed on his face.

"Them niggaz gon' get handled ASAP! I ain't no fuckin' pussy!" Mark fumed and ended the call.

"Never get involved wit' fuck niggaz Mikey... you'll be able to spot 'em from a mile away. Boss niggaz like your big bro are the best," Mark told her as he backed out of the driveway.

"Ugh... why do you keep calling me that?" Micah asked while rolling her eyes.

"You know why... because you always acted like my lil brother instead of my sister, wit' yo lil tomboy ass," Mark said and chuckled.

"Nah yo ass just treated me like a boy so I really didn't have a choice," Micah replied.

"I can't argue wit' that shit, but because of it... I bet you'll always know how to defend yourself," Mark responded.

"Damn right," Micah said as she thought about their most recent trip to the gun range and all of the shit that her brother taught her. It was true; she could defend herself in any given situation thanks to Mark. She hated that damn name that he called her, but he was the only one who could get away with it. Some folks pronounced it as Michael, Mike, and plenty other crazy shit, but Mark's ass was the only person who added the letter "y" to it. Mark pulled up to the school and promised to pick Micah up at the normal time.

"Give me a hug girl," Mark said as she was getting out of the car.

"Aww big brother being a punk today," Micah playfully implied.

"Big brother ain't never a punk... but I just want a hug from my lil brother," Mark told her. When Micah noticed that he was serious, she leaned over and gave Mark a hug. It lasted longer than a normal hug, and neither one of them wanted to let go.

"Go in there and ace that test. I'll see ya later sis," Mark said and forced Micah to let him go.

She headed towards the school and couldn't shake the feeling that had come over her. It was weird and indescribable. Micah texted Mark and told him that she loved him, and he replied by telling her that he loved her too. It was no secret that she and Mark were the closest. She loved Mesha but had a better relationship with Mark. He allowed her to be a part of his street life because he needed her to be well-rounded.

Once the school day ended, Micah walked outside and noticed that Mark wasn't there. She pulled her phone out of her purse and called him several times, but he never picked up. Micah sent him a few texts and those went unanswered as well. She felt like something was wrong. A few minutes after standing in one spot, Micah's phone rang and it was her dad.

"Hi dad... where's Mark?" she got right to the point.

"I'm almost there to get you sweetheart," her dad replied.

"Where's Mark?" she asked again, and felt like something was terribly wrong.

"Come get in the car sweetheart," Mr. Sanders spoke.

It was then that Micah looked up and saw her dad. She walked slowly to the car and got in. Something was wrong and she needed some answers.

"What's wrong?" she asked instantly and her dad sighed.

"Mark is gone," her dad sadly told her.

"Gone? What do you mean gone? Gone where?" Micah asked in a panic.

"He's gone darling... his body was found..."

Micah tuned the rest of her dad's words out. She just couldn't believe what he was saying. Even though she tuned him out, the words never changed. A week later, they had a private ceremony for Mark where only close friends and family were invited. Micah was numb, hurt, pissed off, sad, and every emotion possible. Mark's ceremony was closed casket and she felt like that was a slap in the face. She never got a chance to say goodbye to her brother. From that moment, she vowed to find whoever took her brother away from her and make them pay.

"Who killed him then? If you didn't, you know who did or you wouldn't have his phone?" Micah quizzed after she broke out of her reverie.

"This is gon' sound crazy as fuck… but… Mark isn't dead," Malik told her.

"What kinda games you playing Malik?" Micah asked as she stepped closer to him.

"Put the gun down Mikey!" a voice sounded from behind Micah and she froze.

Chapter 2

Malik's mother used to always say to him, "if you start off with the truth, you'll always win in the end." That was a quote that she lived by and at that very moment in time, he wished he would have listened to his beloved mother. In fact, when Micah first asked him about Mark, he was caught so far off guard he couldn't think straight, so he lied. The shit had been actually fucking with him since that very first day, and that was why he called her to the club. Malik had all intentions on coming clean, but he didn't expect her to come in like Laura Croft and shit, waving a pistol at him.

"Baby put the gun down," Malik pleaded with Micah, although she had turned around and now had it aimed at her big brother, Mark.

Mark looked over at Malik and smirked before he turned his attention back to Micah.

"Remember steady arm baby sis, you'll have a better chance hitting your target," Mark schooled Micah and Malik could tell by the way he said it, that it was just a refresher. He began thinking to himself that Mark had to be the reason that Micah was so knowledgeable about shit.

"What the fuck is going on here? Mark…. How? Malik…" she wailed, shifting the gun back and forth between the two.

"I called you here to talk to you about THIS. And, I know you may be confused but if you put the gun down, I'm sure me and my homie will be able to explain. Just put the gun down Micah," Malik reasoned.

"HOMIE?" Micah repeated after him and Malik could tell that she was still in a daze.

"Yeah, your brother… well Mark is my homie, my friend. We met back in 2010, when he used to hoop at Bells. We became cool and started doing business together," Malik paused and Micah took that opportunity to speak.

"Ok AND…. that's not TELLING ME SHIT MALIK!" she yelled and her voice echoed through the room.

"Man, chill the fuck out and listen…. I know you're hurt and confused but it'll all make sense in a minute," he assured her.

"I'll be the judge of that…. Now continue," she said and motioned with her gun for him to keep explaining.

"Look, I'll continue but you gotta lower that pistol." Malik replied, his anger growing the longer she aimed at him.

"I'm not lowering shit. I don't know what the fuck is goin' on," she snapped and her voice broke a little. Malik could tell that she was now on the brink of tears.

"MIKEY! Do what the man asked you to do, listen for once…. DAMN!" Mark finally spoke up.

Malik figured that it must have been something in Mark's voice that got through to Micah. Or maybe she had grown tired, but whatever it was, Micah slowly lowered her gun and placed it in her waistline.

"Like I was saying, we started doing business together, making a lot of moves. The more moves we made, the more enemies we produced. We got into it with some niggaz from over East and they shot up our blocks, so we retaliated and left all their mothers mourning, except one. One day, Mark was caught slipping, and they sprayed his car at the CitiGo gas station on Roosevelt. Mark wasn't hit but they didn't know that. Them dumb motherfuckers left without even checking to see if he was still breathing. The dudes over East didn't know that Mark was associated with my team, so we collectively agreed that it would be best if he faked his death…." Malik carefully explained.

"FAKED HIS DEATH? THIS IS REAL LIFE, NOT NO URBAN FICTION BOOK. MARK, HOW COULD YOU? Do you know how hurt I was, how hurt I still am behind your death? I based my day to day life on finding out who killed you. You were my best friend. I just can't...." Micah sobbed and then turned to walk out the door, but Mark grabbed her and pulled her into his arms.

"I'm sorry sis, I'm so sorry. You may not understand now but I had to do this. Those niggaz would have came after you, mom, dad, and Mesha next," Mark explained, while his little sister soaked up his Nike shirt with her tears.

Malik stood off to the side and let them have their moment. Micah hadn't spoken much about Mark to him, but just from looking at her breakdown, he knew that Mark must have meant the world to her. He picked up on that early on, but just to see it tugged at his heart.

"Look Mikey, stop all that damn crying. You already ugly. You look ten times worse in tears," Mark joked, which eased the tension in the room.

Micah brought her head up and smacked her lips before she spoke again.

"I missed you so much," she said and placed a kiss on his cheek.

"I missed you too, but I need you to listen to me. Just because I'm here in the flesh, does not mean I can be present. The nigga who so called killed me name is Danny and that nigga been in hiding these two years I been gone. I gotta stay low until we put a radar on that nigga and besides, how Imma explain to mommy and Mesha that I'm actually alive?" Mark said to her.

"Mommy and Mesha, what about Daddy?" Micah quizzed with a stern look.

Mark took a deep breath before running his hands over his waves.

"Daddy cool Mikey," he uttered to her.

"Oh my God! Dad knew about this already?" she yelled.

"I told you it's more to it than you know," Mark replied.

"The only reason I showed up here today was because Malik asked me to. He told me that he fell in love with my big head ass little sister and his soft ass talmbout it didn't sit right with him, keeping this type of secret from you," Mark continued.

Micah darted her eyes at Malik, who stood there with a stupid grin on his face.

"It's ok. I forgive you for damn near killing me… come give a nigga a hug," Malik said, holding his arms stretched out wide.

Micah slowly walked over to where Malik stood and fell into his embrace after a few moments.

"I love you baby, and I'm sorry for not telling you the truth sooner, but it's so much shit I'm trying to protect you from," Malik honestly admitted.

"I can handle protecting myself, but I can't handle you lying to me," she said and lifted her head up and wiped her face.

"It won't happen again," Malik informed her as he removed her hands from her face and kissed the rest of her tears away.

"Good because if I'm going to eventually be the wife of a kingpin, we can't have no secrets… I need in on everything," Micah told him.

"And you got it!" Malik replied and kissed her on her lips.

"Aye y'all cut that shit out!" Mark yelled to them, but they both ignored his ass.

Chapter 3

Rico Grady Jr. weighed in at 7 pounds and 2 ounces, with a head full of hair and rosy cheeks. Goo had never felt so proud, so happy or so accomplished a day in his life. The feeling he felt holding his son was one that words couldn't describe. Goo held his son in his arms and imagined how differently his life was going to be now that he had a mini-him running around. It was at that very moment, he vowed to always be there regardless of what issues Candy or Mona brought his way. RJ was innocent and Goo would protect him from whatever was thrown his way.

"Ok Daddy, it's time to give the baby to mommy for his feeding," The nurse said as she reached for RJ.

Goo reluctantly handed his son to the nurse so Candy could breast feed him. He didn't want to let him go. He felt like this was their beginning to the strongest bond ever. Goo stood to his feet and walked over to the bed where Candy sat up and began to feed their son.

"I think he looks like you," she said, looking up at him smiling.

"Yeah he's definitely my boy," Goo modestly replied.

There was an unsaid rule in the hood, if she ain't yo main, then get a DNA test, but looking into RJ's eyes and knowing the type of woman Candy was, that wasn't even necessary.

"Look baby, I gotta go check up on a few things and change my clothes. Give me two hours max and I'll be back," Goo announced.

"Ok that's fine. My parents and sister should be here by then, and I know they are dying to meet you."

"Cool. Cool. Cool" Goo replied and kissed Candy and RJ on the forehead and then he exited the room. Goo knew that Candy heard his phone conversation earlier, but he wasn't about to go into those details at the moment. He just needed to go handle some shit.

He walked the quiet halls of the Labor and Delivery floor before making it to the elevator. Just as he was about to press the arrow pointing down, the doors opened and a face he wasn't too thrilled to see appeared.

"What's up Micah?" Goo spoke up first.

"Hey Goo…. Just here checking on my girl," she beamed excitedly.

"Aw straight up. Well, she down the hall in room number seven," he instructed and pointed in the direction with his index finger before stepping around her onto the awaiting elevator.

Micah took a few steps forward before turning back around, "Aye! Congratulations nigga!" Micah smiled before the doors to the elevator closed.

To be completely honest, Goo had mixed feelings about Micah, but the fact that she was there for Candy and their unborn son when he wasn't able to be, made him push any other personal ill feelings about her to the back of his mind. And on top of all that, his homie was in love with shorty, so she got extra points off the strength of that.

Once Goo made it to his car, he had a yellow ticket attached to his windshield. Not even giving a fuck about what it was for, he snatched it off, ripped it up and tossed it onto the grass. He drove home in complete silence, something that he only did when he had a lot on his mind and at that moment, he couldn't think straight. Goo thought about his wife at home and that evil ass stunt that she pulled. He also thought about how things would work out between him and Candy now that their son was in the world. The only thing that could calm his nerves at this moment was a hot shower and a blunt, two things that was waiting for him when he got to the crib.

Goo pulled up in the driveway of his two-story home and noticed Mona's car still parked in the same spot. A part of him wished she really would have left, but he knew he still had shit to address with her, so he got out of his foreign whip and headed inside.

The house was quiet as fuck and Goo thought about how people always said "the calm before the storm" well that was the exact case. Goo threw his keys and wallet on the kitchen counter before heading upstairs. The closer he got to the bedroom he shared with his wife, he began to hear noise from the TV. He had no idea how this whole shit was about to play out, but he prepared himself for the worst.

"Mona we need to talk."

When Goo entered the bedroom, he found her sitting in the middle of the bed, Indian style just staring into space.

"Talk about what? Your illegitimate child and his hoe ass momma?" she snapped her neck in his direction and barked.

"Naw… but we will talk about how you and your motherfucking cousin tried to kill them though."

Goo felt his anger growing, the more and more he thought about what she did.

"I didn't have shit to do with that," she replied and uncrossed her legs and scooted towards the edge of be bed.

"BITCH YOU GON' LIE TO MY FACE?" Goo yelled, walking over to where she was sitting.

"I'm not lying Rico, I swear. Yes, I hate Candy and I'm hurt that you have a child outside of our marriage, but I would never try to kill someone. I leave that type of shit up to you," she mused.

"So coincidentally, yo bum ass cousin is Candy's medical assistant one afternoon and then within the next few hours, she's being rushed to the hospital?" he quizzed with his head cocked to the side.

"Look, I told Tammy about the situation, but she took it upon herself to do what she did. I swear to God I wasn't behind that. You know she's my favorite cousin and would go to war for me," Mona resounded.

"Well, going to war for you just got that bitch killed," Goo said and turned away and walked into the bathroom.

Mona jumped up and followed him, "Oh my God Goo, you bet not hurt her.... I swear to God if you do...."

"If I do WHAT?" Goo turned around, his eyes piercing through hers.

"Don't hurt her," Mona pleaded with tears in her eyes.

"I'm telling you now, y'all better start making arrangements. And truthfully, it's taking everything in me not to take your life right along with hers because I know you lying."

Mona grabbed Goo by the arm but he yanked away.

"Bitch let me go!" he spat.

"Why are you doing me like this?" she fell to her knees and cried.

"You did this shit to yourself," was all he said before closing the bathroom door in her face.

After showering for about twenty minutes, Goo returned to the bedroom where he found Mona laying across the bed this time. He couldn't believe what his marriage had turned into. He partially blamed himself because he was the one who had been unfaithful, but the shit she was doing was too much.

"You leaving me again?" Mona asked, lifting her head as Goo got dressed.

"Yeah, I'm going to see my son," he replied nonchalantly.

"But what about me? What about the baby I'm carrying?" she cried, rubbing her flat stomach.

"That baby will be straight too. I'm just not fuckin' with its momma," Goo replied, placing his chain around his neck.

"But Goo...." Mona yelled, but he was already walking out the front door.

Chapter 4

When Micah and Malik finally broke their kiss, she stared into his eyes. Her thoughts were conflicted. Everything that Mark said weighed heavily about her feelings in the entire ordeal, but she briefly wondered if she could really trust not only Malik, but also Mark. Micah turned her head and looked at her brother and they locked eyes momentarily.

"Everything was to protect you baby… and I couldn't tell you no shit like this without having him in your presence," Malik said after he grabbed Micah's chin and turned her head back to face him.

"I believe you… it's just all crazy," Micah admitted.

"I know it is… and I know yo lil ass street smart, but you don't know everything, love," Malik told her and kissed her on the forehead.

"You're right," Micah agreed after several moments of silence.

"Trust me babe… I got you!" Malik replied as he pulled Micah close to him.

After Micah kissed him passionately, she smiled at him. She knew that she already loved Malik, but at that very moment, she knew that she was in love with him. Micah knew that loving someone was totally different than being in love with them. The thought of being in love used to scare her, but as she stared into Malik's eyes, everything just felt so right to her. What she had with Johnathan was no comparison at all to her and Malik's relationship. Micah was willing to continue forward, despite the circumstances, but she knew that she needed to have a heart to heart talk with Mark before he disappeared again. Him telling her that he still couldn't be seen was like a punch to the gut, but just like Malik said, she didn't know every detail of the situation. Something popped into Micah's mind and she began to panic for a moment.

"Damn!" she exclaimed.

"What?" both Malik and Mark asked in unison.

"Candy! She's in labor. She texted me while I was at the spot... I need to go and check on her, but I need to talk to you too," Micah said as she directed her attention to Mark.

"Yeah you need to go and be wit' her... I hope she ain't alone," Malik stated.

"Walk me down to my car Mark... and I got your package down there too," Micah told Malik.

"I'll get it later... you go check on Candy and I'll see you later on," Malik jested and gave Micah one final hug and kiss before she exited his office.

Micah walked out of Malik's office right in front of Mark, but not before she turned around and got one last look at him. No matter who said what, he had still lied to her and that wasn't something that she could forget right away. She planned to move forward but not without caution. Micah wanted to get to Candy as soon as possible, but there was no way that she could leave without talking to Mark, especially since she knew that he was not back for good. That was one of the things that conflicted her the most, seeing her brother but knowing that he was about to disappear again.

"I know all of this is crazy baby sis... but I swear to you, I wouldn't have ever done this shit if it wasn't necessary. And Malik is a good guy... he came through big time for me, or I would really be dead for real," Mark explained to Micah.

"You right, it's all so crazy... how am I supposed to go from thinking you were dead, to seeing you, and then having you disappear again? And mom and Mesha can't know... but what all does dad know?" Micah inquired.

"Sis, the shit is complicated. No, you can't tell moms or Mesha, and dad knows everything. Actually, I think dad got a little deeper into some other shit, but I can't explain what I don't know. Everything we said upstairs, it's the truth. I wish like hell my life could go back to normal, like yesterday, but the reality is, it can't...

at least not yet. It's still one mo nigga lurking and until his head is on a platter, I gotta lay low. I been up in New York… yo big bro been missing you, and everyone else too, but I been making major moves," Mark said.

"How much longer? Are you coming back home or staying in New York when this shit is over?" Micah sadly inquired.

"It all depends baby girl… you know how this street shit works. You just never know," Mark affirmed.

They talked for a few more minutes, and then Micah finally hopped in her car and headed towards Northwestern. Micah used the time that she drove to the hospital to reflect on the day's events. If anyone would have told her that Mark was still alive and that she would see him again, she would have called them a bald faced liar without hesitation. To see her brother and know that he was alive baffled her, but she was consumed with joy. When Micah found Mark's phone, in her mind, she really thought that she was about to have to kill Malik, but she thanked God that everything worked out.

Before Micah knew it, she was at the hospital. She had to drive around a couple of times before she found a parking space because it was just that packed. Northwestern was one of the nicer hospitals, and they were known to have friendly staff. Micah knew that Candy was in great hands, but she was ready to get up there and be by her side just in case Goo's punk ass was missing in action like he had been for the past few weeks. Micah already knew what floor Candy was on, so she hopped on the elevator and headed up. Just as she was getting off, Micah bumped into a familiar face waiting to get on the elevator.

"What's up Micah?" Goo spoke.

"Hey Goo… just coming to check on my girl," Micah replied.

Goo told her what room Candy was in, and Micah headed down the hall.

"Congratulations nigga!" Micah turned around and said to Goo right before the elevator closed.

Micah wondered if Candy had the baby already and if she had, where Goo was going so soon. It wasn't her place to ask him, so she proceeded forward. She knocked on the room door that Goo told her as she slowly eased it open. Micah walked in and saw a nurse holding a baby as Candy sat there smiling, but also looking a little frustrated.

"Awww…. You had him," Micah exclaimed as she walked closer to the bed.

"Yahhsss… about an hour ago and I'm tryna breastfeed, but it's a headache. I'm ready to quit before I even begin," Candy said in frustration.

"It takes time sweetie. You're going to be just fine," the nurse implied sweetly.

Micah watched as the nurse assisted Candy with trying to breastfeed. After a few minutes, he finally latched on a little, but not much.

"Remember, he won't eat much the first few days, and it's normal for him to lose weight… he won't starve, I can assure you," the nurse stated.

"How much did he weigh?" Micah questioned as she stood at Candy's bedside.

"He was seven pounds and two ounces… I was mad to go into labor a few weeks early, but his ass might have been eight or nine pounds if I had of gone to my due date," Candy commented.

"I agree," Micah chuckled.

"I'm gonna take him back to the nursery… you get some rest and I'll be back to check on you later," the nurse informed Candy.

"He's so handsome, girl… Rico Junior?" Micah said as the nurse walked out.

"Yeah, he's a junior... you shoulda saw his daddy's face when I said another name first," Candy replied as she shook her head.

"Speaking of daddy... I met him getting on the elevator as I was getting off. Where he running off to?" Micah quizzically inquired.

"He got a phone call that put him in an uproar before the baby was born, but he didn't leave until now. I didn't ask any questions, but I gotta tell you something though," Candy said as she tried to sit up.

"Be still girl... do you supposed to be doin' all that moving?" Micah frantically asked when she saw Candy moving and making faces that looked like she was in pain.

"I'm okay... but listen. Some bitch gave me a shot at my appointment, and the nurse said that's what put me in labor. Goo said the name rang a bell, so I'm thinking the shit gon' lead back to Mona," Candy explained.

"WHAT THE FUCK? ARE YOU SERIOUS?" Micah fumed.

"Yes... I'm trying not to focus on it right now, but when I find out all the details, that bitch is mine," Candy retorted.

"Not if I get her before you," Micah replied.

"Don't you get all worked up... Goo did look pretty pissed off, so I'm sure he prolly gonna handle the shit before either of us can," Micah continued.

"Hmph... he better!" Candy exclaimed.

"What took you so long to get here though?" Candy asked.

"Girl... if I told you, you wouldn't even believe," Micah sighed.

"Oh damn… it's been a hell of a day for everybody I see," Candy said while shaking her head.

"Well… I was about to… I thought I was gonna have to kill Malik…" Micah started saying and Candy gasped loud as hell.

"I know… let me finish though," Micah said and finally sat in the chair that was by the window.

She ran down the day's events to Candy. Micah and Candy had developed a great relationship, and even though they hadn't known each other for years, Micah felt like she could trust Candy. She really looked up to Candy like she was her big sister. Micah loved Mesha, but they didn't always click too well because of their different choices in life. By the time Micah was done with her story, Candy's mouth was wide open in shock. Candy closed her mouth and then opened it like she was trying to speak, but no words came out.

"I know… you're speechless. Remain that way because we can't let this get out," Micah sighed.

"I need a drink behind that, but I don't think I can drink and breastfeed," Candy said.

"I'll drink for the both of us later," Micah replied and both of them laughed.

Micah pulled her phone from her pocket and looked at the time. She didn't realize that so much time had passed. She saw Candy dozing off and encouraged her to get some rest. Micah informed Candy that she was going to go check on the baby in the nursery, but as soon as the words left her mouth, the nurse walked in.

"I was just coming to see him," Micah said.

"You can hold him before we try to get mama to feed him again," the nursed beamed.

Micah sauntered over to the sink and washed her hands, and then she got the baby from the nurse. She smiled down at him and instantly fell in love with him. She was never even one who thought about kids, but looking down at Rico Junior made her think about having some little ones running around. The baby began to stir a little, so Micah went ahead and handed him back to the nurse, who then prompted Candy for feeding time. Micah's phone began to ring, and she knew by the ringtone that it was Tasha. She answered and Tasha was in a panic.

"Micah... I... I need you," Tasha cried into the phone.

"What's wrong? Where are you?" Micah frantically inquired.

"I'm... I'm... at the... apartment! Please come now!" Tasha panicked.

"I'm on my way!" Micah said and hung up the phone.

"I gotta go check on something, but I'll call you later and I'll be back tomorrow," Micah told Candy.

"Okay girl... thanks for stopping by and keeping me company," Candy told her.

"Stop it... I'll see you soon!" Micah said and left.

She had no idea what was wrong with Tasha, but it sounded serious, so she needed to get to her. Micah knew that her relationship with Tasha had been on the rocks, but the past month or so, things had been semi-normal. She prayed that everything was okay and began to feel a little guilty while thinking that Tasha had gotten into some type of trouble because she had abandoned her. Micah headed to their apartment in silence and made up in her mind to get things back to the way they were with Tasha. She knew that Goo was over Tasha, so as long as Tasha didn't have any ill feelings about Candy, everything would be just fine.

Chapter 5

Tasha left work feeling lower than low. Just when she decided that she was going to cut out her foolish ways, she was hit with an ultimatum she never expected. Tasha normally did crazy shit for a thrill, but to set her friend up for someone else didn't sit right with her. She entertained the thoughts of telling Micah what was going on, but she knew that wasn't an option if she wanted to keep her life. To prove his point before she left, the big black mystery man called out all of Tasha's information to her, including her address, family names, and some other shit that she never told a single soul about. To say that she was stunned would have been an understatement. When Tasha made it outside to her car, naked pictures of her were plastered on the windshield, and when she got inside, she picked up a note and read it.

The words on the letter had her so shaken up that it took her ten minutes just to crank up. Tasha was scared to grab the bag that was on the floor, so she just exited the parking lot and left with no particular destination in mind. Tasha wondered if Micah was at home, so she decided to head there to see instead of calling. She hoped that Micah would be out and about, and that would give her some time to think. Her thoughts were all over the place as she drove and coming up with a plan was even difficult.

Tasha made it to their apartment about fifteen minutes later, parked, turned her car off, and then sat there for a few minutes. She finally took a deep breath and reached over and grabbed the bag that was on the floor. Tasha shook the bag and felt movement, but she couldn't tell what was inside, so she said fuck it and went ahead and opened it. The sight before her was not what she was expecting at all. A small smile crept upon her face as she stared at all of the money that was in the paper bag. It was like the money did something to her, her creative juices as well as her pussy juices began to flow as she finally figured out what she could do to lure Micah all of the way in. Tasha grabbed her cell phone, dialed Micah's number, and went into acting mode as soon as her friend answered.

"Micah... I... I need you," Tasha cried into the phone.

"What's wrong? Where are you?" Micah frantically inquired.

"I'm… I'm… at the… apartment! Please come now!" Tasha panicked.

"I'm on my way!" Micah said and hung up the phone.

"Damn… that was easier than I thought," Tasha said after she ended the call and got out to head inside.

One small part of her thought about telling Micah the truth, but that would end her life, so Tasha decided that she had to do what she had to do to survive. She mentally noted that it was a dog eat dog world, and she decided to be a fucking pit bull. Tasha made it inside the apartment and went straight to the kitchen to retrieve the scissors from out of the second drawer. Since she had on work clothes, it wouldn't be hard to rip them a little bit more and make everything seem real. Tasha didn't want to bruise herself, but she had no choice if she wanted to reel Micah in and gain her sympathy.

Tasha looked in the refrigerator and saw some oranges so she grabbed one, put it in a plastic bag and hit herself in the face a few times. She cursed the entire time that she beat herself. Before she went to her room, Tasha banged her arms in the door and then used a knife to cut herself enough to draw blood. Tasha got most of the idea from what Lynn Whitfield's character did on A Thin Line Between Love and Hate, but it wouldn't be her if she didn't add anything extra to the mix. After she looked in the mirror and was satisfied with her results, she crawled into the bed and closed her eyes and awaited her dear friend's arrival.

Tasha felt herself drifting off to sleep and almost succumbed to it until she heard the front door opening. She heard Micah calling out to her, and once again went into acting mode by sniffling and forcing her eyes to water.

"Tash… I'm here!" Micah croaked as she walked into the room.

"Micah," Tasha moaned as she slowly pushed the covers off of her.

"Oh my God! What the fuck happened to you? We gotta get you to the hospital!" Micah exclaimed as she stared down at Tasha.

"No... I... I can't go to the hospital," Tasha said barely above a whisper.

"What the hell you mean you can't go to the hospital? Look at you all beat up and shit! What happened Tash?" Micah quizzed.

Tasha broke into tears, and Micah sat down on the bed and pulled her close. She cried out as her friend continued to comfort her. After Micah asked her one more time what happened, she finally answered.

"I... I got raped!" Tasha blurted out.

"RAPED?" Micah fumed.

"You gotta get up and go to the hospital if you got raped Tash... the fuck you thinking?" Micah continued.

"I... I just can't Micah! You don't understand," Tasha replied and began crying louder.

"Well let me at least help you get cleaned up. I'll be right back," Micah said and got up and left the room.

Tasha felt accomplished as she watched Micah walk out. She knew that Micah had a heart of gold and would forget about any disagreements they ever had once she laid eyes on her. Another thought popped into Tasha's head just as Micah walked back into the room with two ice packs and some different types of ointment. Tasha winced as Micah rubbed her wounds. The shit really did hurt, and she couldn't wait to heal and get back to herself. She whimpered and really drew Micah on in.

"I really can't understand why you won't go to the hospital," Micah sighed.

"Because they will ask questions that I don't wanna answer Micah... he will kill me if I tell," Tasha responded and forced more tears to stream down her face.

"Who did this to you, Tash?" Micah probed.

"Micah… I don't want you to get involved… besides, I didn't see his face, but I saw a car that was just like his leaving the parking lot," Tasha bawled.

"Tash… who?" Micah pleaded.

"He drives a black Maserati…" Tasha whispered.

"It's only two niggas wit' a black Maserati in the area… Malik… and…" Micah replied.

"Goo…" Tasha finished her sentence.

Chapter 6

Malik drove down Lake Shore drive on his way to Goo's condo that was located in Hyde Park, right off the water. A week had passed since him and his homie sat down and chopped it up. Malik was busy trying to get back in good graces with Micah because she was still hurt behind how everything went down with her brother Mark. She swore up and down that she understood and was over it all, but Malik knew his woman and knew that she was lying. Instead of being at his house all the time like she was before everything unfolded, Micah had been spending all her time at home. She ran some script by him about Tasha needing her, but knowing Tasha, she didn't need shit but money and dick.

Goo, on the other hand, was adapting to being a new father and dealing with shit with Mona. Malik knew for a fact he had his hands full.

Malik: Outside nigga

Malik shot Goo a text and let him know that he was outside his house. It took him damn near fifteen minutes to find a park, which was the only reason he hated going over that way. All the money that nigga paid for mortgage and Goo ain't even guaranteed a parking spot for himself. Malik hopped out of his Jeep truck and headed towards the front door. Just as he was about to ring the bell, Goo swung the door open.

"What up nigga, you look bad?" Malik greeted his homie before Goo turned around and headed back in the house and dismissed him.

"Fuck you! You would look bad too if you was going through the shit I was going through," Goo replied and then flopped down on the cream leather sectional in the living room.

Goo was wearing a pair of jogging pants, a wife beater, and mixed matched socks. His dreads looked like he hadn't touched them in months. Goo wasn't the "pretty nigga" type, but Malik had never seen his homie looking that bad.

"You need to vent?" Malik asked as he walked out of the kitchen with a Miller Lite in his hands.

"Vent? Nigga what I look like a hoe?" Goo screwed up his face.

Malik chuckled at him before shrugging his shoulders.

"Ok nigga, I do need to vent…. These bitches getting on my nerves. Lord, they driving me crazy. So you know Candy had the baby last week right? Come to find out, Mona's cousin damn near killed her and the baby. You remember Tammy thick ass? Well she's like a nurse or sum shit, and she gave Candy some shit to make her go into labor, luckily she made it to the hospital in time. Then, I'm there with her right before she's going into labor and Mona text me talking about she's pregnant. HOW THE FUCK I GO FROM NO KIDS TO TWO? So, I go home to holler at Mona, she tell me that she had no idea her cousin did what she did, but I know she lying man. Now, Candy won't even let me take JR home, but I can't blame her. She's thinking that Mona might hurt the baby, but Mona ain't that dumb. I haven't even been back to the crib in Olympia Fields, I been here all week. Candy and JR spent like four days here. She just went back home last night cuz her people visiting. Mona texting and calling me all damn day. I swear to God, I just want a divorce, take my son, and runaway from all this shit."

Malik listened attentively as Goo broke everything down to him. Micah told him bits and pieces of what was going on from Candy's prospective, and after listening to Goo, both stories were similar. That is the first time in their adult life that his man was going through some shit involving women.

"Damn, that's crazy… you ever thought about reaching out to that bitch who be fixing all these hoes life?" Malik questioned.

"Who?" Goo asked puzzled.

"You know, shorty on TV, you go on her show, talk about your problems and she fix yo shit," Malik broke out laughing.

"Nigga, I'm glad you think this shit a game. Fuck you!" Goo snapped.

Malik couldn't stop laughing. He knew what Goo was dealing with was real, but he wasn't in a position to give any advice because he was still trying to make things right between him and his girl.

"How's Micah's crazy ass doing?" Goo asked, as if he was reading Malik's mind.

"She good man, she's still giving me the cold shoulder though," Malik replied.

"I told yo ass don't tell her about Mark," Good retorted.

"Lying is what got yo ass in the situations you in nigga, so why would I listen to you?" Malik quizzed.

"Motherfucker, you lie because you have to. Mark disappeared for a reason, a reason bigger than HER! What if someone just so happened to have seen him when he came back? And then what? Look, all I'm saying is, you could have told her without having him being present," Goo preached.

Malik understood what Goo was saying and where he was coming from but shit was already done. At that point, him and Micah needed to move forward.

"You right. You right," Malik nodded his head in agreement.

"Aye, you heard anything about Tasha?" Malik shouted out after gulping down the last of his beer.

"Tasha who?" Goo questioned.

"Nigga Tasha. Tasha," Malik reminded him.

"Aw nah, I haven't seen or heard from her since New Year. Why?" Goo asked.

"Nun, Micah told me that she's been dealing with a lot of shit lately. I guess that's her excuse not to be around me," Malik admitted.

"Well if you wanna keep your girl and ensure that she stays a "good girl", you need to try to keep her way from Tasha. You know the saying, 'birds of the same feather, hoe together,'" Goo stated.

Malik burst out in laughter and Goo joined in, but it was funny that Goo mentioned that because that's been something heavy on Malik's mind for a while now. So heavy that he went out and purchased a condo and had it completely furnished just for Micah. He felt that since they had only been together roughly six months, he didn't want to push it and have her move in with him, so he got Micah her own place. He planned on telling her about it soon, but he needed to get all the way back in first. He had been sending her flowers every day, apologizing for the shit with Mark.

"So what you gon' do?" Malik asked Goo as he stood to his feet and prepared to leave.

"I don't know. Candy's cool with co-parenting. I low key don't think she wanna be with me, but I wanna be with her and Mona's the complete opposite. She ain't trying to hear shit other than we gon' be a family and be together but then again, I can't blame her. We've been working for years trying to have a kid, the timing is fuck'd up but that's not her problem," Goo confessed.

"Well big fella, if I was you, I would be with Candy and get a test for your wife's baby," Malik blurted out.

He watched Goo's face as it screwed up instantly.

"I'm just saying nigga, shit sound fishy to me but aye, that's your life," Malik replied, holding both hands in the air as if he was surrendering.

"Yeah, you get the fuck outta my crib," Goo stood to his feet and walked Malik towards the door.

"Aight but for real though bro, think rationally. I'm about to go holler at Micah. I'll talk to you later," Malik said his final words to Goo before heading to his car.

Once inside his ride, he grabbed his phone to shoot Micah a text. Surprisingly, she replied right back.

Malik: Can you meet me somewhere, I have a surprise for you.

Micah: Sure baby, where?

Malik: 122 N Michigan Ave

Micah: Okay!

After he sent the last message, Malik placed his phone in the cup holder and headed to his next destination.

Chapter 7

Shit just wasn't the same for Micah anymore. She tried her best to shake everything off and act like all was well, but it was hard. There hadn't been many things in life that made her feel so conflicted, but the situation with Mark and Malik had been weighing very hard on her. Malik was doing everything imaginable to get back into her good graces, and Micah appreciated it, but deep down, she felt like if she let that lie slide so easily, he would do it again effortlessly. One part of her knew the game because Mark had taught her so much, but the love shit was something totally different. The truth of the matter was, she was in love with Malik Jefferson, and she was smart enough to know that love was sometimes blind.

That situation wasn't the only thing that was on Micah's mind. In fact, it was second because she needed to address one other person and find out what the hell their side of the story was. Micah had just left the apartment where she kicked it with Tasha. The incident that Tasha had gone through really changed her, and it seemed to be for the better in Micah's eyes. It had only been three days, but the change was clear because Tasha hadn't left the apartment and that was so out of character for her. Micah was thankful that she was okay and told her that she would be there for her every step of the way, especially since she refused to seek medical and psychological attention.

When Micah was about five minutes away from her destination, she focused back on the matter at hand. Since she had sent her sister a text before she left her crib, she knew that Mesha was gone out on a lunch date and that worked in Micah's favor. She turned into the funeral home and parked in the back. Micah briefly thought about the shit that went down and shook her head. Little by little, she was reminded of different events and started to slowly connect the dots. Micah got out of the car and headed inside. She had been trying to come up with the correct way to approach the situation, but finally just said fuck it and whatever comes up will come out.

"Hi dad," Micah spoke when she walked into his office and found him sitting behind his desk going through some papers.

"Hi sweetheart! What a nice surprise!" he greeted and got up and gave his daughter a hug and a kiss on the jaw.

"What brings you by?" he probed as he walked back around the desk and sat back down.

"I quit my job and now I'm gonna take back over the books here. Mesha said you've been doing them, and I know you have enough going on," Micah said.

"Oh... uhh, you don't have to do that darling. I just want you to focus on school," Mr. Sanders replied.

"It's the summer dad. I been out of school over a month now, I got it," Micah said and turned to leave.

"Micah... I got it! I've gotta get some things back on track. I can't let you take over when everything isn't together," he stated.

"Dad... it's me! You know I got this!" Micah exclaimed as she stared at her dad as he began to fumble with the papers before him.

"I know that, sweetheart... but let me do this, please," he pleaded with her.

Micah stood there and stared at her dad. She knew that he was hiding shit. She had a good theory too, but she just couldn't confirm anything without looking at the books. Even though Micah hadn't worked at the funeral home in a little while, she knew the business like she knew the back of her hand. It was her dad who taught her, so she knew that by him saying he didn't want to turn it over to her while it was in a mess was bullshit. They had rough patches in the past, but never to the extent of what she saw the last time she snuck and looked at the books. Micah decided to try another approach.

"Do you miss Mark, dad?" she asked after she sat down in the chair directly across from him.

"Or course I do... every single day," Mr. Sanders replied.

"You ever feel like he's alive… because I do sometimes," Micah carefully said.

She didn't miss the expression that her dad gave. Micah captured the image in her mind, and it confirmed everything that she knew and what Mark and Malik explained to her. The only thing that was left untold was what in the hell was her dad doing with his money and why someone dropped bodies off to him around back?

"You love and miss him sweetheart… that's understandable. We all do…" her dad started saying until she cut him off.

"What if he's alive though? Who identified his body? You or mom?" Micah quizzed.

"If Mark was alive, it would be some type of miracle Micah… miracles do happen, but don't work yourself up," Mr. Sanders said and his phone rang. He held his finger up to silence her and stood up as he took the call.

Micah sat there in deep thought when her dad walked out and left her alone. Her plan was just to make comments and see where her dad's head was at. After that short conversation, she pretty much knew. Micah pulled her cell phone out of her pocket and looked at the time. It was almost noon, and she told Candy that she would be there around that time, so Micah got up to leave. She intended on telling her dad that she would see him later, but he was nowhere in sight. Micah proceeded outside, jumped in her car and left.

On the way to Candy's place, Micah commanded Siri to call her mom. Her mom always called her first, so Micah made a mental note to do better and beat her to the punch sometimes. It was Monday, so she knew that her mom was more than likely out and about because she ran most of her errands at the beginning of the week.

"Hi Micah… is everything okay?" her mom asked as soon as she answered.

"Yes mom… how are you?" Micah chuckled.

"I'm in the garden section at Lowe's. I thought something was wrong when I saw you calling," Mrs. Sanders replied.

"Nothing at all… I have a question though," Micah said. She tried to choose her words wisely, but Micah needed to question her mom.

"Go ahead," Michelle told her.

"Did you view Mark's body at the morgue?" she inquired.

"No… your dad told me that it would hurt me more to see him like that, so he wouldn't let me. At times, most times, I resent myself and your father for not following my first mind, but there's nothing I can do about it now. I feel like I never got that closure. I'm sorry, I'm just rambling. Why do you ask?" Michelle said.

"I just been thinking about my brother a lot," Micah admitted.

She talked to her mom for a few more minutes, and finally hung up when she made it to Candy's place. It was rare that her and her mom held meaningful conversations. Micah had always been a daddy's girl while Mark and Mesha were her mom's favorites. That call made Micah see her mom in a different light. She wished that she could tell her that Mark was alive, but she promised her brother that she wouldn't do that. Micah prayed that the next six months would fly by and things would go back to normal.

Micah popped her trunk and then got out after she sent Candy a text and let her know that she was outside. She had all types of gifts for RJ. Since Candy was forced into labor early and Micah couldn't have the surprise baby shower as planned, Micah decided to bring everything to her. It was going to take a few trips, but she loaded her arms with diapers and wipes and headed to the door. The door opened before Micah made it, and she knew that she had to be staring at Candy's father. It looked as if he had chewed her up and spit her out.

"You must be Mr. Williams?" Micah stated more than asked, and he laughed in return before he replied.

"Is it that obvious?" he chuckled as he took the items out of Micah's hands.

"It is… and thank you. I have a few more things to get," Micah told him.

"Nonsense… go on and visit with Candace. I'll get the rest," Mr. Williams told her and Micah handed him her keys.

She walked towards the living room where she heard voices and saw Candy and who she figured was her mom sitting on the couch. They all spoke and Candy introduced Micah to her mom.

"I brought you some stuff… your dad is getting the rest," Micah said.

"Micah… you're just too sweet. These grandparents brought so much stuff… as well as his daddy. Come on let me show you," Candy said as she got up.

"Girl you bounced back quick… look at you," Micah admired Candy when she got up.

"You making me blush… I guess that breastfeeding is helping because I been eating everything in sight," Candy replied as she led Micah to the back.

"RJ is getting so big," Micah said as she reached down and rubbed his chunky thighs before she followed Candy.

"He really is… it doesn't even seem like it's been two weeks since I had him, but it has. When they weighed him at his appointment this morning, he had gained almost two pounds and the doctors were stunned because they said most babies lose weight the first couple of weeks," Candy explained.

"Well… he's a handsome little chunk… how's the pappy?" Micah inquired.

"Girl… he's actually been a big help. I stayed with him a few days but came home before my parents arrived. I won't allow my son to be around his bitch ass wife though. She just might have to see me after my six weeks are up because I found out exactly what happened," Candy fumed.

Micah listened as Candy broke everything down to her. Candy told her that Goo let his argument with Mona slip and Candy was furious. As the story unfolded, Micah became angry as well. She didn't know much about Mona, but she knew that Malik didn't care for her. And as she listened to her friend vent, she could understand why.

"Yeah… that bitch gonna have to pay," Micah seethed.

After that conversation shifted, Candy and Micah started sorting through RJ's things and they talked about everything under the sun. Micah told Candy everything except about what happened to Tasha. She didn't want to think about that at the moment and the thought of Goo raping anyone was still a shock to Micah. He wasn't one of her favorite people, but she still didn't think that he was pressed enough for pussy to take it from anybody. With Tasha saying it was a black Maserati though, Micah didn't know who else it could have been because she knew good and damn well it wasn't Malik.

Micah's phone chimed with a text, and she pulled it out and saw that it was Malik. She smiled because Candy had just informed her to move forward and try not to dwell on that one lie. Micah read his message and replied back. She was a bit confused as to why he wanted her to meet him on Michigan Avenue, but she wrapped up her time with Candy, took a few pictures of RJ, and then left.

Twenty minutes later, Micah pulled up at the address that Malik had texted her. Micah had heard about Michigan Ave Condo's, but she had never been there. If she was a baller and wasn't on a budget, she would gladly live there. Just as she picked up her phone to call Malik, his picture popped up onto her screen.

"Get out baby," he said as soon as she answered.

Micah looked up and saw Malik standing at one of the doors.

"How many places this nigga need to lay his head?" Micah mumbled to herself as she got out of her car.

She jogged towards Malik because it was hot as hell.

"What are you doing here?" she asked.

"Come on… I wanna show you somethin'," he told her and grabbed her by the hand.

Micah watched him as he unlocked the door and followed behind him. Her mouth hung open as she admired the beauty of the condo that Malik led her through. Micah began to notice that the place was furnished with things that she talked to Malik about before. The teal colored sectional was a dead giveaway because she mentioned upgrading her furniture, and he asked her what kind she wanted. As they walked through the place, one part of Micah was in awe because she knew that Malik had purchased the place for her, but the other part felt conflicted because she didn't know if he was trying to control her every move or not. When they finished the walk through, Malik handed her the keys.

"It's all yours baby!" he beamed.

Micah stood there for a few minutes weighing her options. She didn't know what to say. She didn't want to seem ungrateful, but she also wanted to maintain her independence to a certain degree.

"What's the catch?" Micah asked, and when Malik didn't answer right away, she knew that he had an ulterior motive.

Chapter 8

Goo laid across the bed listening to what sounded like Mona dying. She was in the bathroom throwing up for like the hundredth time that morning. He stayed the night over at the home they shared together because it was the day of her first doctor's appointment. They were still on bad terms, but Goo knew it would be fucked up of him had he not been present. It wasn't like he had ill feelings towards Mona because after all, she was still his wife. He was just caught up in a bad situation that didn't seem like was going to get better anytime soon.

Last night, before he dropped Candy and RJ off, he thought about telling Candy about Mona's pregnancy, but decided to keep it to himself for a little while longer. Part of the reason was because he didn't want to hurt her, and the other part was contributed to the fact that he wasn't sure that Mona would actually be able to carry the baby full term. It sounded harsh, but those were facts. It was the fourth time she'd been pregnant, and each time resulted in a miscarriage. Goo figured, why get Candy all worked up for no reason if the same thing happened again.

"Ok let me grab my purse and then we can go," a tiresome looking Mona said walking out of the bathroom.

Goo got up and stretched before walking behind his wife and down the stairs of their two-story home. Goo stood in the doorway of the kitchen while Mona grabbed a banana and a bottle of water from the refrigerator.

"Aight let's go baby!" she chirped, while she threw her purse over her shoulder and headed out the door.

Goo got inside his black Maserati and headed out west to UIC. He didn't understand why Mona chose that clinic for her primary care when there were so many other facilities near their home. They drove the entire way listening to Jay-Z old album The BluePrint," rapping along occasionally. Goo let Mona out at the door and circled around to find a park. Luckily for him, on the second trip around, a couple was leaving out of their spot right by the door. Goo backed in the parking spot, let his windows up, and hopped out. It was summertime Chi, the best season when it came to activities around the city. Despite the dry heat, it was his favorite season as well.

When Goo entered the clinic, Mona sat near the window on the phone, filling out some paperwork on a clipboard. She quickly ended the call before his ass could even touch the seat.

"Who was that?" Goo questioned.

"My crazy ass sister," she replied and then stood to her feet and took the paperwork back to the front desk.

Goo didn't bother responding instead he just took his phone out of his pocket to read some of the unseen text messages that was in his inbox. He had a few from random bitches, a couple from his workers, and one from Candy that he opened first. Through the preview of the message, he could see that it was an image. When he finally retrieved the message, Candy had sent a picture of RJ smiling in his sleep. The sight of his son caused him to beam unknowingly.

"Fuck you grinning for?" Mona blurted out, while standing in front of him.

"Aw its nothing," he replied nonchalantly and then saved the photo and placed his phone back in his pocket.

"No nigga its' something and I wanna know," she insisted.

Goo shook his head before letting out a loud sigh. "Candy sent me a picture of our son," he finally admitted.

"Aw for real, let me see," she said excitedly before taking a seat.

Goo hesitantly pulled his phone back out of his pocket and went to the picture.

"Here," he mumbled and handed her the phone.

Mona stared at the picture with a blank stare before quickly handing it back to Goo.

"What?" Goo quizzed because he could tell by the look on her face, she was feeling some type of way.

"Nothing," Mona shrugged.

"Aight," Goo replied and let it go.

"Naw I think he's a cute kid. Don't look shit like you, but cute kid nonetheless," Mona affirmed.

Just as Goo was about to snap, a nurse in a pair of pink scrubs appeared from the back and called Mona's name. Her and Goo stood to their feet without saying a word and walked to the back of the clinic where the rooms were located. Once inside, that same medical assistant gave Mona instructions on how to pee in the cup and where to leave it. Mona left out and went to the bathroom while Goo waited around, replying to the other text messages that he hadn't had the chance to.

"Ok, the doctor will be in with you two in a few minutes," the medical assistant informed them before exiting.

The two of them sat in the room quietly. Both of them browsed through their phones before Mona spoke up first. "Boy or girl?"

"Huh?" A confused Goo replied.

"Boy or girl, which one you want?" she asked more precisely that time.

"Aw... I guess a girl," he stated and looked up at her briefly and then back at his phone.

"Whatever Rico," she retorted and rolled her eyes.

"What the fuck is your problem man?" he snapped.

"I don't have a problem. I just want you to be as happy as I am. My name must gotta be Candy for that shit to happen huh?" she grimaced.

"I ain't come here to argue you with or discuss another motherfucker," he snapped back.

"I aint trying to argue either Goo, I'm just saying…"

"SAYING WHAT?" he cut her off.

"I'm just saying… if it's a boy, it damn sure can't be a junior because that's already taken," she grunted.

It took everything in Goo not to get up and leave her ass there by herself. He was sick and tired of her, always talking about the same shit. Either accept it or don't and move on were his true feelings.

The doctor came in shortly after their small altercation and spoke with Mona about the pregnancy and the risks that time around. They listened to the baby's faint heartbeat and after that, the doctor told them she was rounding out to be about six weeks pregnant. The previous pregnancy lasted until she was twelve weeks. They had hope that she would be able to make it out of the first trimester this current time.

After setting the next appointment, they left and headed to grab lunch since the both of them was starving. Once inside the car, Goo got another text message from Candy, saying that RJ was so greedy that he was trying to hold the bottle by himself already. Candy started off breastfeeding, but she wasn't producing enough milk for his chubby ass so she had to stop. While Goo replied to the message, Candy FaceTimed him out of habit, and he connected the call without thinking.

"Where you at?" Candy's voice echoed throughout the car, causing Mona's neck to snap around.

It was at that very moment Goo knew that he fucked up. It was too late to hang up and it would have been rude as fuck had he.

"On my way to the crib," he replied, looking back and forth at his phone and then the road.

"Aw ok baby, I wanted to show you how JR was holding this bottle, but I don't want to distract you from driving. I'll record it and send it to you. Call me when you park," Candy replied.

Without responding to her, Goo just ended the call and that's when all hell broke loose. Mona shifted all the way around in her seat and just stared at him. Goo knew that she was about to spazz the fuck out by the look on her face.

"YOU THAT BOLD NOW, MUTHAFUCKER? YOU ANSWERING THE PHONE FOR YOUR SIDE BITCH WHILE I'M IN THE CAR?" she screamed.

Goo glanced over at her briefly before focusing back on the road.

"Yes, I did Mona. Anytime that phone rings, it could be regarding my son, therefore I have to answer. The same goes for you, when you have my princess," he stated calmly.

"Ok, I get that, but nothing distinguishes me from her and that's the problem," she relaxed a little and said.

"That ring on your left hand is what separates you two. I don't know how many times I have to remind you that you are my wife. I'm not sure how many times I have to apologize. I've never told you this before, but you are leaving me no choice…either forgive me or file for divorce. Those are your options. My son is here and Candy is his mother and ain't no way around that. I'm not finna keep reminding you of my fuck-ups. The ball in your court," he said mater of factly.

Mona sat there in silence, like she was lost in transition before she finally replied.

"I'll be damn'd if I let a bitch take my place. Through sickness and health, until death do us part, but I do have one request."

"What's that?" Goo quizzed.

"You arrange a sit-down between the three of us. I gotta set some shit on the table," Mona demanded.

Chapter 9

Since Micah was at her parent's house, Tasha used the time to go and meet up with Bear. It hadn't been as easy as Tasha thought it would be to stay on the straight and narrow and continue playing the role to win all of Micah's trust back because Bear called and texted constantly while she played her role. One week while they were watching a movie, Tasha thought that Micah had saw a text message from Bear by the way her mood suddenly changed, but after probing, Tasha found out that wasn't the case at all. Micah told her that she was conflicted about a situation. After Tasha acted concerned, she learned that Malik had purchased a condo for her. Micah smiled as she spoke about the condo, but then turned sad when she said that she didn't want to leave Tasha alone during her most vulnerable state. Tasha told her that she was fine. However, she planned to put something else on Micah's mind when she made it back home later.

Tasha pulled up at Uncle Remus where Bear instructed her to meet him an hour ago and saw a blacked out Escalade and knew that it was him. It wasn't the same vehicle that she had saw him in before, but just by looking at it, there wasn't any doubt about who was behind that dark ass illegal tint. She parked in the first space that she saw and then headed towards the truck. When she heard the locks click, it confirmed that Tasha was right, so she went around and hopped in the passenger seat.

Wap!!

Tasha rubbed the left side of her face after Bear smacked the shit out of her.

"What the fu…" Tasha started saying until Bear cut her off.

"You don't have me waiting no muthafuckin' hour. Don't you know I got shit to do," he spat.

"Look… I'm playing the role. Micah is a smart ass bitch and if I move too soon or the wrong way, she gon' know my ass is back up to no good. You gotta let me do this my way," Tasha fumed.

"And hitting ain't part of the deal... I'm helping you, nigga!" she continued.

"I don't know who the fuck you think you talking to, but you better take that shit down ten notches. We both know you ain't loyal to nobody but ya got damn self and if it wasn't for them racks I broke off, you woulda tried to find a way outta this. Let's get this shit straight... I don't need you, but I want you because you the best one for the job. You jealous of your so called friend anyway so the shit works out perfectly. Now, what info you got for me?" Bear said and then lit a blunt and hit it twice.

"Nothin' yet... she will be back home soon and Ima see if she wanna go to the mall. I got a plan I'm working on," Tasha told him.

"You got three days to bring me some info... three and that's it!" Bear asserted.

"I got you," Tasha affirmed.

"Now lean over here and suck the skin off daddy's dick!" Bear gloated and leaned his seat back and closed his eyes.

Tasha wasted no time granting his request. She hoped that when she was done, he would let her ride it because she needed to feel a dick in each of her holes badly. After she sucked him off and swallowed his cum, Tasha sucked Bear hard again and then removed her panties and hopped on his shaft. She was happy that she wore a dress for easy access.

Ten minutes later, Tasha headed back to the apartment and prayed that Micah hadn't made it back yet. Luck had to be on Tasha's side because she didn't see Micah's car when she pulled back up. She was able to get some dick and if her plans worked out with her friend, it would be one of the best days that Tasha had in a while. After sitting in the car for about five minutes scrolling on Facebook, Tasha heard a knock on her window and almost jumped out of her skin.

"What the fuck?" she asked as she stared at Mo, after opening the car door and making her way out.

"You just been doggin' a nigga huh… what the fuck you on?" Mo badgered.

"It ain't even like that baby… I been low key because… because…" Tasha started talking, but she burst out crying midway through her sentence.

Mo pulled her in and hugged her tightly and coaxed her to tell him what was wrong. Tasha knew that Mo had a soft spot for her by the things that he said and did for her. Ever since they hooked up at the bar, got drunk as hell, and then fucked each other's brains out, Tasha had him wrapped around her fingers. He shared his true feelings with her like she was his ride or die chick, and Tasha happily played the role just in case she needed him. The time had finally come, she needed him, but too bad for him she needed him gone. Through her fake tears, she knew just how to make him disappear, permanently. Tasha told Mo through tears the exact same story that she told Micah. Since he had confided in her his hate for Malik and Goo, she knew that Mo would try to go and take Goo out. Tasha also knew that the duo that he was trying to go up against was too smart for Mo. At times, Tasha wondered why Malik hadn't killed him yet, but with the information that she had just given him, his life was on the clock.

"Answer the phone when I call you. Ima handle that nigga before this week is out!" Mo told her and disappeared.

Tasha went inside of her apartment and laid on the couch. A few minutes passed and she picked up her phone to call Micah, but she heard the door knob being fumbled with and Micah walked in a few seconds later.

"I was just about to call you girl," Tasha beamed.

"I planned on being back before now, but my mom just didn't want me to leave. She's gotten a little clingy lately and that's hella strange," Micah said and Tasha noticed the distressed look on her face.

"Is everything okay?" Tasha queried.

"She said it is, but I'm not so sure… anyways… aren't you tired of being cooped up in the house?" Micah said and then changed the subject.

"Yahhsss… I was gonna see if you wanted to go to the mall," Tasha said.

"Sure… let's go," Micah replied and Tasha hopped up.

Ten minutes later, Tasha was in the passenger seat of Micah's Maxima singing the lyrics to Bad and Boujee as her friend maneuvered the street in route to Rosemont Outlet. Tasha figured that they should shop first, eat, and then on the way back, she would pick Micah for any information that would be useful to Bear. They made it there about twenty minutes later and the fun began. It had been a while since Tasha had been shopping, and she was about to put a dent in the money she received the night that she signed her soul over to the devil.

Tasha bought three pair of jeans, a few shirts, and a couple pair of heels and called it a day. She didn't know what all Micah had purchased, but she had quite a few bags as well. On the way back to the car, Tasha struck up a conversation.

"Do you think Malik is tryna control you by making you move?" Tasha carefully asked.

"Control me? Nahhh… at first that did pop into my mind, but after I thought about it, I realized that he was just tryna make me happy," Micah replied.

"You think he faithful to you? A man of his status gotta have hoes running around… seem like he tryna control you to me and I don't want you getting caught up," Tasha hinted.

Before Micah could answer Tasha, Micah's phone rang and Tasha smiled inwardly. She made a mental note to dig up any dirt on Malik that she could. Tasha knew that he had to have some type of secrets that could be dug up to destroy him and turn Micah against him. Micah popped the trunk and threw her bags inside and Tasha followed suit. Tasha could tell that she was engrossed in an important conversation by the look that was on her face. As they got inside, Micah crunk up and a few seconds later, the call connected to the Bluetooth and Tasha heard some shit that she knew would make Bear happy as fuck. Micah switched the call back to her phone and Tasha pulled out her phone and sent a text.

Bear: New shipment going to 16th and Homan Thursday!

Chapter 10

Malik stared at the ceiling and thought about life and how much shit was changing day by day for him. He had become a man at a young age and a boss by default. He wondered how things would have turned out if his mother was still alive. Would he still be in the streets? Would he be rich or would he be just one of those regular square ass niggaz? He then looked over at the beautiful woman lying on the side of him and smiled. Never in a million years would he have thought that he would be in love. In love to the point where he was cutting all the women before Micah off. Sure, there was Nina and she was no doubt his world, but Micah made him feel a different type of way. The thought of Micah alone made his dick hard. He debated on whether or not he should wake her up out of her sleep for some pussy, but remembered how he fucked the shit out of her the night before, so he figured he would give her a break for once. Micah shifted slightly in her sleep. Malik adjusted his body, offering his arm for her to use as a pillow. Micah snuggled close to him before opening her eyes, cracking a warm smile.

"Good morning baby! What time is it?" She asked in a groggy voice.

Malik playfully frowned up his face before placing his hand over his nose, indicating that she had morning breath. Micah laughed before biting his arm. She hopped up and ran to the bathroom that was connected to his bedroom. Malik could hear the water running and her gagging a few times, and he knew she must have been washing her face and brushing her teeth. A few moments later, she returned to the bed and crawled right back under him as if that's where she belonged.

"Now what was you saying Pam?" Malik laughed, referring to a character from his favorite TV show Martin.

"You got all the jokes this morning huh? But I was asking what time was it? Why you up so early?" she questioned.

"Well beautiful, if you must know, it's after eleven and I only been up for maybe twenty minutes," he informed her.

"Damn, I didn't know it was that late. I must have been sleeping good," she replied as she leaned over and grabbed her cell phone off of the night stand closest to her.

Malik looked over her shoulder as she scrolled through Facebook. He didn't have an account himself, so he had no idea what the fuck was going on in the world of social media. It just wasn't anything that he wanted to be a part of.

"What that hoe talking about?" he asked when Micah clicked on Tasha's page.

"Stop talking about my damn friend," she fussed before reading a few of Tasha's statuses while Malik followed along.

Malik shook his head at the shit he was seeing, niggaz and bitches like Tasha were the reason he stayed clear of the internet because it was a fantasy world. You could be whoever you wanted to be behind that screen and the real world would have no idea. Malik looked away briefly when he heard his phone vibrating on the floor. He told Micah to rise up momentarily while he retrieved it. Once he grabbed it, it stopped ringing but he noticed it was Goo calling, so he immediately called him back. Goo answered on the first ring and by the way he was breathing, Malik knew something was wrong.

"My nigga, you need to get out west ASAP!" he fumed into the phone.

"Aight but why? What up?" he quizzed.

"Aye remember that shipment? That big ass shipment that came through this morning. Well it's been hit. A motherfucker robbed the crib on 16th and Homan," he roared.

"Wait. Wait. Wait. How? Only a handful of niggaz knew about that move," Malik fired back.

"Exactly! That's what I'm trying to figure out," Goo exclaimed.

"Aight man, I'm on my way," Malik replied before ending the call.

He quickly got up and began getting dressed. He was fuming on the outside, but tried his best to remain calm on the outside.

"Everything ok?" Micah asked, sitting up in the bed.

"Nah, some shit happened at one of the traps. I need to get over there ASAP!" he explained.

"Ok baby, I'm going to Taste of Chicago today with Tasha, just call my phone if you need me," Micah told him.

Malik paused what he was doing and stared at Micah. He wanted to say something about her still hanging with Tasha, but figured now wasn't the time, so instead, he nodded his head in agreement and headed out the door.

The entire ride to Holy City, he thought about his team and how he hand-picked everyone with the help of Goo. Malik started to think that there was a mole in his camp, and he had to figure out who it was, even if that meant clearing house. About thirty minutes later, Malik pulled up behind Goo's car, parked and killed the engine before stepping out. Out of habit, he checked his surroundings and went up the stairs of the two flat building. Malik paid for the building in cash, using an alias name. They kept the maintenance up, ensured that the grass was cut, and snow shoved in the winter. They had a florist to come out and plant flowers in the summer as well. Riding pass the building, you would definitely think that the building was occupied by a family.

"LOOK AT THIS SHIT!" Malik yelled out in frustration as soon as he entered the living room.

The place was vandalized and on top of that, three of his workers were stretched out with gun shots to their head. Malik looked up and Goo entered the living room with his pistol in hand.

"Any idea?" he questioned.

"Nope but I'm about to get some answers," Goo replied.

Malik knew that Goo lived for shit like this, gunplay was his hobby, and usually Malik was the voice of reasoning but all that reasoning shit went out the window.

"What they take?" Malik nervously asked.

"Everything my nigga, except the safe that's in the shower walls," Goo told him.

"See! That alone let's me know it was an outside hit. Everybody that knows about this spot knows about the shower. This had to be done by someone who didn't know or else, that would have definitely grabbed that too," Malik explained.

"Either that or the motherfucker wanted to make it look like an outside job so they purposely left it untouched," Goo countered.

"You right," Malik nodded his head in agreement while stepping over a body, heading towards the kitchen.

"Aye, you called the clean-up crew?" he yelled out to Goo.

"Yup, they on their way!" his partner replied.

"Aight cool, now let's figure out who all knew about this shipment," Malik said, joining Goo back in the living room with a bottle of water.

"Shid, that's easy, everybody in this room," he stated, pointing to the men lying dead on the floor.

Malik scratched his head before sitting on the armrest of the black sofa.

"Nah man, it has to be more to this. You sure you ain't tell nobody else?" Malik pondered.

"Nigga I'm sure, are you sure?" Goo shot back.

Malik sat there for a moment and thought about it. He was usually careful about anything and everything concerning their business. He had spoken with the workers yesterday evening, after leaving the barbershop. He then called Micah to see if she wanted something from Portillos. It was then that he realized he told Micah about the shipment, but he knew Micah wouldn't go run her mouth about it. It was more to the story but he knew where to start, so he pulled out his phone to give her a call.

Chapter 11

As soon as Malik left, Micah decided to get on up and get dressed. She had new clothes at his place that he had bought for her, so the only thing she had to do was dress and go pick up Tasha. It was hot as hell outside, so Micah decided on a white romper. They would be doing a lot of walking, so her gold flats by Steve Madden would be perfect for the day. Micah turned on the shower and then went and grabbed her phone and sent Tasha a text. Surprisingly, Tasha replied back instantly.

Micah: I'll be there in forty-five minute tops! Be ready slow ass!

Tasha: Bitch, Ima be ready! You just bring ya ass!

Micah laughed at her friend. She really hated that Malik didn't care for Tasha because she wanted the two of them to get along, but as long as they didn't have to be in each other's presence often, it worked for Micah. She knew that Malik wanted her to cut Tasha off, but she just couldn't up and do that because he didn't like her. In Micah's eyes, that would be foul as hell. Micah grabbed two towels and then reached up and opened the cabinet that was above the toilet to retrieve some body wash. Just as she grabbed it, her phone fell into the toilet.

"Fuck!!!" Micah swore as she reached in and got it.

"Got dammit... I should've gotten the water proof case," she continued to vent as she tried to dry her phone off.

Micah hit the power button, but it didn't come back on. She said fuck it and got in the shower with hopes that it would be dry and miraculously start back working by the time she was dressed and ready to go. Micah washed and rinsed her body three times before she turned the water off and got out. The hot water felt so good cascading down her body that she didn't want to get out, but Micah was one who always liked to keep her word, so she stepped out of Malik's magical shower for the time being and dried off.

Fifteen minutes later, Micah was dressed and ready to go. She said a silent prayer that her phone was restored, but when she picked it up, it was still dead.

"God wasn't thinking bout my ass with that prayer," Micah mumbled and grabbed her phone and put it in her cross over purse anyway.

As promised, she pulled up at her place with three minutes to spare, parked and went inside after she turned her car off and hit the lock. She knew that she was going to have to wait on Tasha's slow ass for at least another thirty minutes. Micah used her key to go inside. Upon entrance, she called out to Tasha as she headed towards her room.

"Give me ten minutes!" Tasha yelled.

"I knew yo slow ass wasn't gon' be ready," Micah told her while playfully rolling her eyes.

"I texted and told you not to rush, but you didn't reply. I'm almost done for real," Tasha said.

"Ugh… I dropped my damn phone in the toilet. It's dead," Micah fussed.

"Damn… my ass would be fuckin' crazy without my phone," Tasha said as she applied the finishing touches of her makeup.

"Yo ass crazy WITH your phone… now hurry up. You know it's about to be crowded as hell. Everybody be waiting on July to roll around for this event," Micah said as she walked out of Tasha's room and went to check on some shit in her room.

"I got a homeboy that can fix your phone for the low," Tasha said as she walked into Micah's room.

"For real? I need it fixed because this damn phone is new and I ain't tryna cop another one. Plus, I got a lot of shit in here that I need," Micah said and began to think about the shit she had stored in her phone.

Since all of the crazy shit happened with Mark being alive, Micah had the crazy idea to write a book about it. Of course, she would sell it as fiction, but the shit would be real as hell. She had a few notes saved already and planned on reaching out to an author that lived in Chicago by the name of Patrice Balark. Micah had actually scoped out her Facebook page and she seemed like she was cool as hell judging by her posts, but she wanted to have a solid plan before she asked an expert for guidance. She handed Tasha her phone because she was sure it wasn't going to come back on, and they headed out.

"You want me to drive?" Tasha asked.

"Nah, I got it. Yo ass probably don't even have gas and that means we'll have to stop and be even later," Micah replied.

"You know me so well," Tasha chuckled and hopped in the passenger seat after Micah unlocked the doors.

Thirty minutes later, they arrived at their destination and it was packed as they figured. It was nothing compared to the turnout a few years back, but it was still crowded nonetheless. Since niggaz didn't know how to act, they had begun shooting and shit, so the older crowd elected to stay at home. Micah loved attending and made the decision to just attend in the day time. She knew that it didn't matter whether it was day or night for folks to act fool, but she figured she had a better chance of catching the sane crowd during daylight.

Taste of Chicago was one of the world's largest food festivals that was held for five days in July in Grant Park. They always had live music on multiple stages, including the Petrillo Music Shell, pavilions, and performances. Micah's parents introduced them to the event at young age, and she hadn't missed it since. After they parked, both of them headed straight towards the festivities. Micah was starving, so the first stop she made was to get a deep dish pizza and a drink.

"I feel so lost without my phone," Micah whined as she waited for her food.

"Ima have to use yours to call my baby in a few," she continued.

She saw Tasha roll her eyes, but she ignored her. There wouldn't be any problems unless Tasha actually told her no when she asked to use it, and Micah couldn't see that happening. They got their food and started walking around as they ate. The atmosphere was pleasant, the music sounded great, and it appeared that everyone was having a good time. Micah found some seats near one of the stages and sat down. She noticed that Tasha seemed to be more into her phone than anything, but she shrugged it off. Before they knew it, two hours had passed and Micah asked Tasha to use her phone.

"How long will it take your friend to fix mine?" Micah inquired after Tasha handed her the phone.

"It won't take him long at all. I'll text him when you done talking," Tasha teased.

Micah flipped her girl the bird as she dialed her man's number.

"Hello," Malik answered with frustration etched in his voice. Micah knew that something had gone down with his business, and apparently it wasn't fixed yet.

"Dang... shit must still be bad," Micah stated instead of speaking.

"I been calling yo phone for the past hour... you still at the park?" Malik inquired.

"I dropped it in water, but yeah we still here. What's wrong?" Micah questioned.

"I need you to meet me somewhere ASAP. We gotta talk face to face," Malik informed her.

"Okay, meet me at my apartment in twenty," Micah said and hung up.

"Everything okay?" Tasha asked when Micah handed her the phone back.

"I don't know, but let's go. I gotta meet Malik," Micah said as she stood up.

"Aight… it's hot as fuck anyway and 'ol boy said if I bring your phone later, he can get to it right away," Tasha told her.

Micah heard her, but she didn't really hear her. Something was off with Malik, and she wouldn't be able to rest until she knew what it was. Tasha was engaged in a phone conversation as they headed to the car. Micah heard her tell whomever it was that she was glad they had her back, but once again, she didn't entertain her. She crunk and peeled out as soon as they got in the car.

Fifteen minutes later, Micah pulled into their complex and she parked in her normal spot, got out, and went inside.

"Girl you ain't say shit the whole ride. You okay?" Tasha asked her as they headed inside.

"Something just ain't right Tash, but I'm sure everything will be fine."

When they walked in, Tasha went to her room and closed the door, and Micah kept walking and proceeded to hers. She heard Tasha tell her that she was about to step out in a few, so she mumbled okay. Before Micah could lay across the bed, someone knocked on the door and she knew that it was Malik, so she got up to answer before Tasha. The first thing that Micah noticed were the lines on Malik's forehead, so she knew that he was in deep thought about something.

"Come on, let's go to my room and talk," she said as she grabbed his hand and led the way.

Malik wasted no time getting to the point after the door was closed.

"Is your hoe ass friend here?" he asked her.

"Malik, I told you to stop talking shit about my friend. What the fuck did she do to you anyway?" Micah fired back.

"She a hoe, Micah… why you wanna hang around wit' a known hoe beats the fuck outta me!" he exclaimed.

Micah heard a door slam, and she figured it was Tasha leaving.

"Is this why you came over here?" Micah inquired.

"The trap got robbed. The only people that knew was me, Goo, and three of the workers, and you. Three of the workers dead. I know you didn't tell nobody, but was anybody around you while we were talking?" Malik asked her.

Micah stood there in deep thought before she replied.

"No… wait, Tasha was with me and the call did transfer to Bluetooth while we were talking, but she wouldn't tell anybody," Micah defended her friend.

"Micah… come on now! That bitch!" Malik spat as he paced the floor.

"Tasha wouldn't do that shit, Malik! Cut the bullshit and try to figure out what really happened.

"Micah you gonna have to stop hanging around that grimy bitch! She ain't no fuckin' good!" Malik fumed and headed towards the door.

"You hang with a fuckin' rapist so what's the difference?" Micah yelled and Malik stopped in his tracks.

"What the fuck you talmbout?" Malik turned and asked.

"Goo raped Tasha!" Micah exclaimed and Malik laughed.

"Raped? That bitch be slangin' that pussy faster than mu'fuckin' traffic speed down the Dan Ryan. Rape… Micah you believed that?" Malik asked her.

She watched as Malik pulled his phone out, but instead of answering him, Micah walked to Tasha's room. Right when she walked in the hallway, Micah heard the front door close.

"Tash!" she called out to her and ran to the front door, but by the time she made it, Tasha was gone.

"Goo you ain't gon' believe this mu'fuckin shit," Micah heard Malik on the phone.

Chapter 12

After the clean-up crew left the trap house on 16th and Homan, Goo got in his car and peeled off. He had to send a message to the niggaz on his team, there was no way they should ever be caught lacking like those niggaz got caught that morning. Goo figured since he was already out West, why not slide to their other spot on Chicago Ave and Hamlin. Goo took the streets there and headed right down Pulaski to Chicago Ave. When he pulled up on the block, it was packed as usual. The kids were out playing in the streets, while the dope boys invaded the corners. Someone had even cut the fire hydrant on, on the next block.

Once Goo passed all the commotion, he parked his Benz four houses down from the trap and hopped out. He went to his trunk and pulled out a black Nike hoodie, threw it on, and tossed the hood on top of his dreads. He checked his waist for his pistol and eased down the street. Once he made it to the house, he skipped up the stairs, turned the door knob, and like he expected, the door was unlocked. Goo shook his head and proceeded down the short hall to where the living room was located. He heard voices coming from around the corner, so he removed his gun and cocked it back before entering.

"YALL NIGGAZ WILLING TO DIE OVER 2K?" he yelled, holding the pistol in the direction of the three dudes sitting on the couch.

All three of them looked shook and to say that they were caught off guard was an understatement. Goo removed the hood from off his head and a sigh of relief covered all of their faces.

"Y'all see how easy that shit was? I could have splattered y'all brain all across this motherfucker. Are you niggaz asking to die? Because that's what it seems like to me. The fuckin' door unlocked. Niggaz in here "ha ha he he-ing" like some bitches. IT'S FUCKN WORK IN THE BACK!" Goo screamed out in frustration.

Goo started to secure his gun in his waist, but stopped.

"I should just blow all y'all brains out and recruit some more niggaz," he threatened, placing the gun back on them.

One of his workers Stevo spoke up first.

"Shid Boss, that's our bad. Mo came in to use the bathroom and must have forgot to lock the door back."

Goo interest piqued the moment Mo's name was mentioned. He hadn't heard from him nor seen him since the incident at the club on New Years. He was no longer on their payroll and since the nigga been laying low, he forgot about his existence.

"Where that nigga at?" Goo asked, placing his pistol in his waist.

The moment Stevo opened his mouth to answer, Mo's voice was heard from behind Goo's back.

"I'm right here nigga!"

Goo turned around to see Mo aiming a silver Glock .45 at his head. That wasn't the first time Goo had a gun pointed at him, and he was pretty sure it wouldn't be the last. Not an ounce of fear ran through his blood. However, fear was written all over Mo's face and he was the nigga with the advantage. Goo knew that Mo was a bitch, but he was surprised that he had the balls to pull a stunt like that.

"What you gon' do with that Mo?" Goo asked, taking a small step towards him.

Mo looked down at Goo's feet then back at him before replying.

"Nigga Imma kill you, that's what the fuck Imma do."

Goo chuckled lightly and cracked a smile.

"Kill me for what nigga?" he questioned.

The sound of a phone ringing interrupted their conversation. Mo fidgeted a little before going into his pocket with his free hand and retrieving his phone.

"I'm getting ready to handle this pussy ass nigga right now. Let me call you back," Mo boasted, before ending the call and placing the phone back into this pocket.

Goo wondered what that call was about, but Mo spilled the beans before he had time to investigate.

"Nigga you think you can just rape my bitch and walk around like shit cool?" Mo yelled.

Goo's faced instantly screwed up because that nigga sounded stupid.

"Rape? What bitch? Who bitch? Yo bitch? Nigga you sound dumb," Goo replied, waving him off.

"NIGGA DON'T FUCKING MOVE!" Mo screamed, his sweaty hands gripping the cold steel.

"Bitch ass nigga shoot me then. Fuck we doing all this talking for? I know if somebody would have raped my bitch, all this lip singing shit wouldn't be happening," Goo roared.

Mo's hands began to shake and that's when Goo knew he had pulled his hoe card. If Mo wanted to pop him, he would have been dead already. Everybody knew Mo ain't have no heart and that's exactly why his life was about to end.

"Who is your bitch anyway?" Goo asked, trying to distract Mo the best way he could.

Although Goo knew Mo was a pussy, he also knew if you backed a motherfucker in a corner, they would do anything to get out that bitch. That was why he had to play the situation smart.

"Tasha nigga!" Mo finally answered, with a hint of pride in his voice.

"TASHA!" Goo repeated before bursting out in laughter, causing the other three workers that were still on the couch to laugh as well.

Goo knew the laughter was the distraction that he needed. He noticed Mo's eyes shifting back and forth from him and the other men. Goo took that opportunity to grab his gun swiftly and put a single bullet in the middle of Mo's head. The sound of the pistol going off caused everybody in the room to jump except Goo. Goo then turned around and in a blink of an eye, put a bullet in each and every one of the workers behind him. He realized that he needed soldiers on his team and those niggaz were only weak links. When Mo up'd his Glock, then they should have up'd theirs without hesitation. Instead, they sat there like some little hoes. Goo knew Malik was gon' have some shit to say about what just happened, but Malik was the least of his worries right then. Having to shut down two trap houses and finding a way to reroute this work was top priority for him. Goo looked around the room at the dead bodies before pulling his phone from his pocket.

"I got more work for y'all. Clean up needed on Chicago Ave and Hamlin," was all he said before ending the call and walking out the door.

Goo sat in the car until the crew got there, listening to Young Jeezy's album "Thug Motivation" and looking through his phone. He came across a picture of RJ and smiled before pulling off at full speed. About forty-five minutes later, he pulled up to Candy's crib and hopped out the car. He rang the doorbell once he made it to the door. To his surprise, Candy answered immediately, as if she was looking out the window waiting for him. She stood at the door in an Adidas sports bra and a pair of Adidas leggings with their son sitting happily on her hip.

"What are you doing here?" she asked with a sexy grin.

"I came to see my family," Goo replied, reaching for RJ who practically jumped into Goo's arms.

"Un huh whatever, come in, you are letting my air out," Candy stated before walking off and leaving Goo and RJ standing at the door alone.

Goo played with his son for about an hour while Candy showered and went over some papers for a case she was working on. RJ was almost three months and developing his own personality each day. Goo loved being around his son and being present for those milestones. He was also thankful for Candy. She had sacrificed so much since being a mother, and that was why he planned on doing something special for her, real soon. The more and more they co-parented together, the more he fell in love with her. He still hadn't told her about Mona being pregnant. He was a bit surprised that she hadn't found out herself yet, especially with all the bullshit that be happening on Facebook.

After feeding RJ, Goo went upstairs and laid him down in his crib. He sat there in a rocking chair that was alongside his bed for about another ten minutes before leaving. While heading back downstairs, he walked past Candy's bedroom, peeked his head inside, and got a view of her as she laid across the bed. Goo cracked the door open a little more, just enough for him to slide his skinny frame through without alerting her. He made it all the way over to her bed without her noticing. Goo raised his hand in the air to smack her ass, but before he could land on his target, Candy spoke.

"You touch my ass and Imma fuck you up!" Goo chuckled lightly before taking a seat on the edge of her bed.

"What's up baby daddy?" she asked, sitting up Indian style next to him.

"Shit baby momma, just coolin' how I be coolin'," Goo replied.

"Yeah, we all know what that mean," she shot back.

Goo ignored her last statement. He knew replying could lead to a conversation that he wasn't trying to have at this moment, so instead, he just stared at her.

"WHAT?" Candy shouted, playfully rolling her eyes.

"Look Candy, I gotta tell you something," he said, changing the mood completely.

"What?" she asked, her voice instantly filled with worry.

Goo let out a deep sigh before giving her his full attention.

"Why haven't you let me fuck since your six weeks been up?" he asked in a serious tone.

Candy placed her head in both hands and shook her head.

"Nigga is THAT what you had to talk to me about?" she asked.

"Yeah, what type of female DON'T let the baby daddy fuck?" he quizzed.

"A real one motherfucker…. Especially one who's baby daddy is married," she snapped.

"You can't hold that against me," he responded.

"You sound stupid. YOU married her."

"Yeah, but you can't keep throwing that in my face….. I married the wrong one," he said, mumbling the last part but the look on Candy's face, let him know she heard him anyway.

The both of them sat in silence for a while. Neither one of them not sure of what to say. Goo meant what he said. He wished he hadn't married Mona, but it was too late and her being pregnant was only trapping him more and more.

Ding. Dong.

The sound of Candy's doorbell buzzed through the house, causing her to jump to her feet.

"Are you expecting somebody?" Goo questioned.

"Ummmm yeah. I wasn't expecting you actually and forgot I was having company," she replied nervously.

"Who?" Goo asked, standing to his feet, trailing behind her down the stairs.

Candy walked to the front door and stopped. She turned around and damn near collided with Goo, who was on her heels.

"Look Goo, I been meaning to talk to you …."

"Talk to me about what?" Goo asked cutting her off.

The doorbell rang again and the suspense was starting to piss Goo off, so he reached around Candy and snatched the door opened. Standing at the door was a nigga in a Gucci shirt, a pair of denim jeans, and air force ones, holding a bouquet of flowers. The look on all three of their faces was identical, but Goo was the one shocked the most. Noticing the tension in the air, Candy stepped in between the two men.

"Goo this is my boyfriend Trey, Trey this is RJ's father Goo."

Chapter 13

Tasha stood outside of Micah's door listening to her and Malik argue. Part of her wanted to run in and hug Micah for standing up for her, but the other part of her told her that she better haul ass before Malik walked out and put a bullet through her skull. When Micah brought up the rape incident, Tasha knew that it was time for her to get the fuck out of dodge. She knew that it would only be a matter of time before shit hit the fan, and she planned on being long gone. If things worked out with Mo taking care of Goo like she anticipated, Tasha knew that she could keep her lie going with Micah and keep her on her side.

When there was a brief moment of silence, Tasha knew that someone was about to come looking for her, so she speed walked to the door. She heard Micah calling out to her, but Tasha never looked back. Her purse and overnight bag swung back and forth as she sprinted to her car and hopped in. If Flo Jo would have been chasing Tasha, she wouldn't have caught her because she ran just that fast to her car and hopped in. Tasha started her car, threw it in reverse and damn near hit someone as she backed up. She heard someone screaming and figured that they either hit or kicked the car by the noises she heard. Tasha thought about flipping them the bird, but she elected to just go ahead and leave without causing any more trouble.

Ironically, "Move Bitch Get Out The Way" by Ludacris came on the radio as Tasha turned out of the complex, and she couldn't help but to sing along while laughing. Once she felt she was in the clear, Tasha pulled her phone out and placed a call, and he answered after the first ring.

"Hey boo," she cooed.

"I'm getting ready to handle this pussy ass nigga right now… Imma hit you back!" Mo told her.

That was music to Tasha's ears and she smiled after she ended the call. She knew that one of them was about to die, but it didn't matter to her which one it was. It would work out for the best if it was Goo, but deep down she already knew that Mo didn't stand a chance. As soon as Tasha placed her phone down, she heard it chime with a text, and she got wet as she read it.

Bear: Let me get some of that bomb ass head baby! Meet me at the spot!

Tasha: I'll be there in an hour big daddy!

It was only a matter of time before Tasha had Bear eating out the palm of her hands and she couldn't wait. She was not only putting in work to help him take over Malik's organization, but she was also giving him the best dome that he had in his life. She knew that by the way his body reacted to her. It was if TI was talking about her when he said "brain so good coulda swore you went to college!" she did go, but truth be told, Tasha didn't do shit but fuck and suck, and she was perfectly fine with that.

As promised, Tasha made her way to Terrance's little shop and parked her car. He was a square that she met on campus who took a liking to her and Tasha was able to get him to do her assignments and everything just for a little attention. Of course, she gave him more than attention because that's just who she was. Tasha got out and sashayed inside and found Terrance sitting at his make shift desk. When she made it over to him, she saw his little pecker poking through his khakis and smirked. After she felt him up a little bit, he quickly went to work on Micah's phone and had it restored within thirty minutes. Tasha gave him a kiss, told him thanks, and let him know that she would be in touch soon and then exited.

After grabbing a Big Mac meal from McDonald's with a Hi-C orange drink, Tasha headed towards Bear's spot and pulled up twenty minutes later. Just as she approached the driveway, a car was leaving that looked very familiar, but she couldn't tell who was driving. She cursed herself for being a minute too late because she wanted to know who else that nigga was fucking with. Tasha knew good and damn well that she wasn't the only one, and she wasn't tripping, but it was always good to know who the competition was.

Right before she could knock on the door, it opened and Tasha walked right on in. The first sight she saw was Bear's back, so she happily followed behind him. He sat down on the chaise, laid back and pointed to his dick. Tasha knew what time it was so she went to work as if she needed a place to stay. In reality, she did which was why she sucked him dry, swallowed all of his kids, and then told him what was on her mind.

"Imma need a place to crash for a lil while! Shit done got real!" she said and began sucking him back to life before he could reply.

Chapter 14

Two Months Later

School was back in session, and although Micah still had good grades, she wasn't as focused as she normally would be because of everything that had been going on. She hadn't seen or heard from Tasha since the day they went to Taste of Chicago. Micah called Tasha's phone for three days straight after that day, and on the fourth day, the operator said the number had either been disconnected or changed. She ended up going to get a new phone, and the tech told her that she saw where all calls and text messages ceased for a few hours, but they picked back up later that night and the phone had been used for a few hours. Micah didn't know if Tasha had her phone or if she had left it with the guy who was supposed to be fixing it. The fact that she never got his name didn't help the situation at all.

Micah sat in Micro Economics class trying to put everything together. To some, the shit may have seemed easy, but Micah liked to look at things from different perspectives. She knew that sometimes Tasha could be shady at times, but there wasn't a single thing that Micah could think of that would cause her to be shady towards her. She had searched high and low for her friend, only to come up empty handed. Micah had a discussion with Malik about the rape allegations after he talked to Goo, and to her, Goo was a little too nonchalant. The next time she saw him, she planned on questioning him because he could have very well made Tasha disappear, permanently.

"Your quizzes are due tomorrow night by midnight... don't forget to login before then and submit them. You all are free to go," Dr. Moore stated to the class.

Micah was shocked as hell because Dr. Moore had a reputation of never canceling classes or letting students out early. Micah didn't know the reason for her being so gracious, but she didn't complain. She grabbed up her Vera Bradley bag and left. As soon as she stepped out of the building, she spotted Johnathan with his arms wrapped around some girl. Micah was actually happy for him. That was the first time she had seen him in months. Her smile was short lived when she spotted him walking towards her. The look on the girl's face that was with him was not a pleasant one.

"Why do you still have my number blocked?" he asked as he approached her.

"Don't you have someone to entertain?" Micah asked, while pointing to the unknown female that Johnathan had just abandoned.

"She's oaky… I wanna know why you still treating me like shit?" John inquired.

"Have a great day Johnathan," Micah said and started walking away.

"I saw your girl Tasha leaving my buddy's shop a couple months back," he said and that caused Micah to stop in her tracks.

"Have you seen her since?" Micah quizzed.

"Johnathan, you're not about to sit here and keep disrespecting me by talking to this bitch!" the girl walked up and intervened.

"Bitch? Who you calling a bitch?" Micah mused as she directed her attention to the girl and took a step towards her.

"You! I'm just calling it like I see it," the girl countered.

When Micah moved again, Johnathan stepped between the two of them. Disrespect was one thing that Micah didn't tolerate and with her prior frustrations, anything could make her snap out. Before she could say or do anything else, Johnathan pushed the girl away as she screamed at him about not taking up for her. Micah shook her head and called them both pathetic. As she walked off, she remembered that Johnathan didn't get a chance to tell her if he knew anything else. She told herself that she might have to unblock him and reach out to him. That wasn't anything that Micah wanted to do, but the reality was, she was damn near desperate to find out what happened to her friend. When she called Tasha's mom and found out they hadn't heard from her, it made her suspicions grow even more.

Micah was done with classes for the day, so she headed to her car. She didn't have much of an appetite, so she decided that she would just go to her condo and rest. Since Tasha was gone, and the place Malik bought her was closer to school, Micah went ahead and moved in. The lease at her old place actually ended in August, but Micah paid for two more months just in case Tasha showed up. She didn't want her not to have anywhere to go when she returned, but she sure as hell hoped that she popped back up before September was out because she had fallen in love with her new place. Malik had really outdone himself with everything.

Micah's phone rang as soon as she put the car in gear, and she knew who it was by the ringtone.

"Hey baby!" she spoke.

"What's up sexy?" he replied and she could hear the smile in his voice.

"That voice of yours just instantly got me wet and changed my entire mood," Micah chirped.

"Oh yeah… come on by the club and let me make it that much more better then," Malik challenged her.

"I'm on my way!" Micah cooed and disconnected the call.

Micah smiled as she thought about what was about to go down. Although shit had been intense in the street, and she had her issues, they never let that interfere with their sex life. Micah could literally think about Malik at the drop of a dime and bust a nut, which was why she was about to do eighty in a sixty mile zone to get to his sexy ass. She needed to release some stress, and the best way to do it was to have a few orgasms.

Almost twenty minutes later, Micah pulled up to Club Escape. She used the key Malik had given her and walked in the back door. She knew that more than likely Malik was upstairs in his office, so that's where she headed. Just as expected, Micah found her boo thang sitting behind his desk busy working. The desk was full of papers, but that didn't stop her from walking behind it and then knocking everything to the floor in one swift motion.

"I always wanted to do that shit!" Micah exclaimed with a smirk.

"You crazy as hell," Malik chuckled as he pulled her close to him.

"Un uhh… I'm running this show," Micah told him as she unbuttoned his pants, remove his semi erect penis, and then let her mouth do the talking.

"Got damn girl!" Malik moaned as Micah deep throated his now rock hard shaft.

She enjoyed pleasing her man just as much as he enjoyed receiving. The fact that they always went above and beyond to give each other pleasure made their chemistry a thousand times better. When Micah felt his dick as it began to pulsate, she knew what was next, but she wanted to feel it inside of her wetness so she got up. Her initial plan was to ride it, but since she had made such a dramatic entrance and knocked shit off of his desk, she decided to make use of it. Micah removed her clothes and then laid back on the cherry oak desk. She waited on Malik to enter her, but she felt his tongue instead. The way that he was eating her, Micah couldn't stop herself from grabbing Malik's head and fucking his face.

"Let that shit go… I know what you doin", Malik said as he inserted two fingers into her soaking tunnel and caused her to cum instantly.

"You make me sick nigga," Micah moaned.

They had a little game they always played to see who would cum first. Micah lost the majority of the time, but she had gotten the best of Malik on quite a few occasions. After he made her cum for the second time, he slowly entered inside of Micah's love tunnel and she moaned and groaned at the feeling. It didn't matter how many times they had been together, Malik had to always enter her slowly because he was just that thick. As soon as Micah relaxed, she started throwing her pussy back at him.

After Malik flipped Micah over and entered her again, they both came simultaneously a few minutes later. Micah couldn't move once they were done. Her pussy was still throbbing and she wanted to lay there for the rest of the day. But, Malik smacked her on the ass and told her that he had a few people coming for a meeting soon, so Micah forced herself to get up. She walked to the back corner of the office and followed Malik to his bathroom, where they both washed off. Malik made some small talk about some shit that was going on, and then he asked her if she had found her friend Tasha. Micah told him no, and her mind began to wonder again. She couldn't wait until she saw Goo.

There was a knock at the door a few minutes later, and Micah told Malik that she would see him later; right after he told whomever it was to come in. She leaned down and kissed him, and when she looked up, Micah locked eyes with Goo. Her blood began to boil, but she knew that she had to play it cool.

"What's up Micah?" Goo spoke.

"Really nigga? You know you don't like my ass so cut the shit!" Micah uttered.

"I don't like your hoe ass, lying ass friend," Goo shot back.

"Where she at Goo? I know you did something to her," Micah spat and Goo laughed.

"Maannn… fuck that bitch!" Goo replied.

"You can't even answer, so I know you did it. As soon as I find…" Micah started saying until Malik cut her off.

"Micah… this ain't the time!" he sternly stated.

"You better get your punk ass friend. He just fuckin' over all my friends!" Micah said and then rolled her eyes and left.

"Imma get to the bottom of this shit!" Micah said to herself as she left and headed to her parent's house.

Micah wanted to reach out to her brother so bad, but she didn't want to risk getting him caught in any kind of way. Mark had called her a few times from a burner phone, but the calls were always less than a minute. Most times, Micah didn't know which was worse, thinking he was dead and not being able to talk to or see him, or knowing he was alive and still not being able to talk to or see him. She felt like her back was against the wall, but she had no choice but to pray that the next six months would fly by. The only way she would reach out to him on the number that was in Malik's phone would be if there was an emergency. Micah knew that it might have been wrong of her to even get the number out of Malik's phone, but in her defense, she felt like it was only fair and she had yet to use it anyway. Micah pulled up to her parent's house, but when she saw Johnathan's car in the driveway, she backed out and went to her condo.

Chapter 15

Mona stood in the bathroom mirror, staring back at her reflection while rubbing her protruding belly. She had just gotten out of the shower, dried off, and put on a cute yellow and white maternity outfit she had picked up from Nordstrom's. Her sew in was freshly installed and the Brazilian body wave bundles she had bought from her beautician a year ago, still looked fresh as hell.

"Didn't you tell me to be ready by one? It's damn near two o'clock and we still here," Goo yelled from the bedroom.

"Don't start no shit, Rico. I'm coming," Mona fussed back after she applied some lip gloss.

She put her earrings on and walked out of the bathroom a few minutes later. They were about to head to her doctor's appointment, and she was excited because she hoped they would be able to tell her the sex of her baby. He or she kept their legs closed the last time, and the doctor wasn't able to see a damn thing. Mona remembered fussing and saying that her child was going to be stubborn just like his damn daddy.

"Damn... your belly grew overnight didn't it?" Goo quizzed after she finally exited the bathroom.

"No, it didn't grow overnight. If you did more than mope around, you would notice this kinda stuff," Mona snapped back.

"I can see what kinda day this bout to be," Goo mumbled and walked out of the room.

Mona wanted to call out to him, but she fought against it. Instead, she just grabbed her Birkin bag off of the dresser and headed downstairs. Truth be told, she was tired of arguing with her husband and wanted things to be back how they once were. At times, she wondered if too much damage had been done for them to be happy again. Mona was one who always fought for what she wanted, so she made up her mind to do just that.

By the time she made it outside, Goo was already in the car, so Mona made her way to the passenger side and got in. She stared at her husband and thought about all of the reasons that she fell in love with him and smiled.

"What you got up your sleeve?" Goo asked her as he put his car in reverse and backed out of the driveway.

"I love you, Rico Jefferson, and I want our marriage to get back to how it was. Without all of the arguing and shit. Can we just go back in time? We are about to have a little one looking up to us in just a few months, and we need to practice doing better before I give birth," Mona told him.

There was a long pause before Goo opened his mouth to respond. Mona watched him as he opened and closed it a few times, but she decided to remain silent as he gathered his thoughts. Goo had been in a fucked up mood for the longest, but he never told Mona why. She just snapped at his ass every time he got smart with her and went about her way.

"I love you too, Mona… but shit will never be the same. A lot has happened… almost too much, but I am willing to make the best of this. You gotta realize that I have a son, and Imma be there for him whether me and his mama rocking or not. I'm not dealing wit' the unnecessary drama about me taking care of my seed," Goo finally spoke.

It was Mona's turn to be quiet for a moment after Goo said what he had say. She despised the fact that Candy had Goo's first child. She knew that he cheated before, but for him to fuck somebody raw and get them pregnant, and then have a baby was a lot for her to deal with. She knew that if she was serious about making it work and keeping their family together, then she had to swallow her pride and deal with it.

"I understand. I still told you that we needed to have a sit down, and that has yet to happen. You gotta do your part too, Rico," Mona countered.

"Imma make it happen. I only been dealing wit' Candy about my son. Nothing more, nothing less," Goo told her and Mona couldn't help but to smile.

Before she knew it, Goo was turning into the parking lot, and they were right on time for her appointment time which was at two thirty. Mona sat there as Goo got out, and when he looked back and saw her still in the car, he made his way to the door, opened it, and helped her out.

"Thank you!" Mona cooed and wrapped her arm around Goo's.

They walked inside and Mona was all smiles. She felt like things were finally about to get back on track, and she was more than ready. She had been through hell and high water with Goo, and she planned on being with him forever. After she signed in, she took a seat and pulled her iPhone out and scrolled through Facebook. Mona had joined a few groups and started gathering ideas on a baby shower theme. She couldn't wait to start putting everything together. Her only hold up had been finding out the sex of the baby, and she prayed that she knew within a matter of minutes.

"Miss Jefferson," a nurse called from the door, and Goo got up.

"Come on… they calling you," he told her when Mona didn't move.

"Miss Mona Jefferson," the lady said, and Shamona finally got up.

"It's MRS. Jefferson," Mona said when she made it to the door.

She wouldn't have paid it much mind if it wasn't the same nurse that flirted with Goo on her last appointment. Mona saw right through her bullshit, and she wasn't there for the games. The nurse smirked before she handed Mona a cup and told her the same thing she did at every other appointment. Mona snatched it from her hands and went to handle her business. When she was done, she washed her hands, walked out and found Goo in the next waiting room.

Five minutes later, her name was called and they were led to an examination room. Mona was happy the wait wasn't long and that was why she loved her doctor; he didn't overbook his patients. The nurse asked Mona the routine questions, and then handed her a gown to put on and instructed her to lie down and get comfortable. Mona did as she was told and she rubbed her belly as soon as she laid down. A few moments later, Goo was beside her, and he placed his hand over hers. She could tell that he wanted to say something by the expression that was on his face, but he remained quiet and so did she.

"Mrs. Jefferson, how are we doing today?" her doctor asked as soon as he walked in.

"Just fine," Mona smiled and replied.

"Seems like everything is going just fine. You're twenty-five weeks pregnant now, and we're going to see if we can detect the sex. Maybe we will have some luck this go round," the doctor said as he placed the monitor on her stomach and they listened to the heartbeat. The baby had a very strong heartbeat, and Mona just couldn't believe that she was really about to be somebody's mama. After everything that she had been through, shit was getting real and a part of her was nervous as hell.

"Well... well... well... looks like the two of you will be welcoming a little junior in a few months," the doctor stated as he pointed at the screen and showed them.

Mona's heart sank a little because she wanted a girl since Candy had already given her son her husband's name. She wanted to say something, but she put on a front and smiled like she was the happiest person in the world.

"A junior he will be!" Mona exclaimed as she locked eyes with Goo.

It took everything in her to remain calm. They had taken two steps forward and Mona vowed to not let her be the cause of them going backwards again. Her doctor printed off the ultrasound pictures, handed them to her and gave her his normal speech, instructing her not to do too much and to call if she had any questions whatsoever. When he left the room, Mona got up and put her clothes on quietly. She didn't utter a word as she slipped her clothes back on, and neither did Goo. Arguing hadn't gotten them anywhere in the past, so Mona figured maybe shutting the hell up would. She exited and made her way to the checkout out window. After Mona scheduled her next appointment, they left.

"I guess I can start planning his baby shower," Mona said after Goo crunk up and left.

"Yeah… you can do it however you want to," he somberly replied.

Before she could say anything else, his phone rang.

"What up?" he answered.

"I'm not far from there, I'll swing through," Goo said and hung up.

"You hungry or you want me to take you home? I'm 'bout to meet Malik at Bar Louie," Goo told her.

"Yeah I'm hungry," Mona replied.

She rotated between Pinterest and Facebook as Goo maneuvered his way to Bar Louie in Oak Park. Mona knew that money wasn't an option so she was about to put together the baby shower of the century. Mona sent out text messages to her closest friends and family with the good news. A short ride later, Goo turned into the parking lot. He drove near the door and dropped Mona off while he went and parked. Mona took that opportunity to send out a few more texts with a picture that she had snapped of the sonogram.

When Goo walked up, they went inside. Mona followed him as he walked to a table in the back. She did a double take when she saw Malik and his girl. Mona didn't know that they were joining them. If she did, she probably would have declined because she knew that Micah went on the trip with Candy and Goo. Just by looking at Micah's face, Mona knew that she was shocked to see her as well. For that reason alone, she decided to stay. They sat down and a waitress came and took their drink orders right away.

Goo was engrossed in a conversation with Malik, so Mona broke the ice by striking up a conversation with Micah.

"When these two get together, it's always some craziness," she said and chuckled in reference to their men.

"How far along are you?" Micah quizzed as she looked at Mona's belly.

"Twenty-five weeks!" Mona beamed and rubbed her belly.

"Wow! You're pass the halfway mark," Micah noted.

The waitress came and took their orders, and then Goo told Mona that he would be right back before him and Malik got up and left. Mona thought it was sweet how Malik gave Micah a kiss because she hadn't seen him show any woman any type of emotions in years. The more she thought about it, Nina was the only woman she remembered Malik talking about until Micah came along.

"I know you don't know me, and I don't know everything about you either… but I can't sit here and act like we cool. I don't like what you did to Candy. You could've killed her and her baby. You sitting here pregnant yourself, so I would think you would know how it feels to have a life growing inside of you," Micah stated.

"What happened to Candy wasn't on me. I'm very sorry with how everything played out, but that was all my cousin's doing because I vented to her. I can understand your frustrations as a friend, because I would be pissed if I was in your shoes. I plan on telling Candy the exact same thing very soon," Mona expressed.

She watched as Micah relaxed a little after she said that, so Mona decided that she would open up to her a little more.

"I've been through a lot with Goo. More than anyone will ever know, but I love my husband to death, and we are trying to make our marriage work. I know your friend probably hates me, but Goo loves his son, and we really need to be able to get along for the sake of the child. You seem like you have a good head on your shoulders, so maybe you can talk to her," Mona continued.

"I don't get into other people's business like that, but I will say this, Candy is very smart," Micah replied and took a sip of her drink.

Mona shifted the conversation to her baby shower and made small talk about it until their food arrived. When the men returned to the table, sports talk took over and Mona sat there thinking that everything was going to be alright. In her eyes, it had to be, or there would be hell to pay.

Chapter 16

Since Goo decided to handle the trap house situation his way, Malik left it up to him to fix the bullshit that he created. Malik couldn't understand for the life of him why Goo's mind worked the way it did. He was the shoot first, ask questions last type of nigga and regardless of how many times Malik reminded him that dead niggaz can't talk, Goo still did shit his way. Since the street shit was handled by him now, Malik had more time to focus on other things like Micah and his club.

Micah had been staying at the condo that Malik got for her, and he was ecstatic about that. Their relationship was going well and Malik had been thinking about making shit official with her and by official, he meant "before God." Although they had only been dating for almost a year, he felt like he wanted to spend the rest of his life with her. He figured they could be engaged for about a year or two and then take that leap down the aisle. His only concern was Micah's age, she was young as fuck, but you wouldn't be able to tell from the way she acted.

Malik sat at the bar at the club, looking over a clipboard that contained the liquor inventory. That was something that his assistant Monica usually would do, but since she was out of the country for a week, Malik filled in for her. Everything looked good in his eyes. All of the orders added up, but he couldn't wait to be done with the tedious shit so he could head home. He had a migraine that wouldn't leave for shit. After finalizing the last order, Malik pulled his phone from his pocket and shot Goo a text. They planned to meet up at the spot after he was done at the club, but Malik told him to just come to his crib instead. After Goo replied, he placed his phone face down on the bar and stood to his feet. He headed up stairs to grab some money out the safe and lock up.

Once he made it to his office, Malik went inside the hidden compartment located in his desk drawer, entered the code and pulled out the stack of money that was inside. Malik then closed and secured the safe before walking around to the front of his desk, where he took a seat and counted the cash. A knock at the door interrupted him. Without raising his head and losing his concentration, he told the visitor on the other side to "come in".

"You know you look even sexier with money in your hands," a female voice sounded through the room.

Malik stopped counting his money and eyed the person who had just entered his office. In front of him, wearing a pair of leggings and a crop top, with a pair of laced up red bottoms, stood Jayda. Jayda bit her bottom lip before walking closer towards Malik. Jayda and Malik used to mess around before he met Micah and even in the beginning stages of their relationship, but when Malik decided to get serious with Micah, he cut Jayda off. Jayda reached out a few times after that but with Malik curving her, she eventually got the picture and gave up.

"Fuck you doing here?" he finally asked.

"Well, I was riding pass and seen your car out front. I knew had I texted or called you, you wouldn't have answered, so I decided to just show you what you been missing instead!" she replied seductively.

Malik laughed a little before placing the money he had counted in his pocket.

"Shorty, I ain't been missing out on shit, but ummmm... nice seeing you though," he nonchalantly replied.

Jayda made a sad face, pretending to be hurt before walking closer. She completely invaded Malik's personal space. She stood directly between the small gap between his legs. Malik couldn't front, Jayda was indeed a bad bitch, but he also knew she was nothing but trouble. The time they shared together was cool, but she was never the type he could settle down with. She didn't have it in her.

"So Malik, tell me what or who got you playing me to the side like I'm a lame?" she inquired.

Instead of answering her question, Malik just stared at her with a smirk on his face. He wanted to tell her ass to leave, but those full glossed up lips had him thinking something different.

"Well you may not be thrilled to see me, but HE IS," she said, referring to his now semi erect dick that was beginning to bulge out of his pants.

Jayda reached down and grabbed his manhood without warning, but it didn't cause Malik to react. His reaction came from his already opened office door and an awaiting Micah who stood in the door way. The look on Micah's face was similar to the look she had a few months back when she thought he had something to do with her brother's death. It was a look of hurt, a look of betrayal. Without warning, Malik pushed Jayda away from him, causing her to stumble a little over her heels. When she finally gained her composure, she looked at Malik for an explanation, but he was lost for words.

"Malik, I'm not understanding, what bitch got you tripping on me like this?" Jayda questioned again, and he knew that she was completely unaware of Micah standing behind her.

"I'M THE BITCH THAT GOT HIM TRIPPING LIL MAMA!" Micah stated, her voice causing Jayda to turn around.

Jayda looked Micah up and down before bursting out in laughter like she was at a Kevin Hart comedy show. Micah shifted her weight to one side, placing her hand on her hip, and Malik knew by that stance that she was ready to wrap up all that giggling shit.

"Aw wait, you serious…. She serious huh Malik?" she asked, turning her attention to him now.

"Look Jayda, you might wanna leave while you can," Malik warned her, but it was already too late.

Micah had already walked around the two of them and placed her purse on the desk. She then came in between the space that separated Jayda and Malik and faced Jayda.

"Look, this can go one of three ways. You can leave and never reach out to my man again or you can say something smart that'll get yo ass beat, orrrrrrr… you can say something REALLY REALLY smart and get yo ass popped. And as you may know already, if it comes down to option number three, you know my man can make one call and have you erased. But the ball is in your court my dear…" Micah snapped.

Jayda's eyes shifted back and forth between Malik and Micah as if she was weighing her options. Malik stood behind Micah shaking his head "no" trying to warn Jayda. She must have caught his drift because without saying a word, she flipped her hair and exited the office. A sigh of relief escaped Malik's body, but he knew it was far from over by the way Micah turned around and stared at him.

"What the fuck was that about Malik?" she hissed.

Malik shook his head before explaining.

"I use to fuck with her before you came along. I cut her off. She showed up here because she seen my car out front," he told Micah.

"Why the fuck you wasn't answering your phone then?" she questioned.

"Baby I left my phone downstairs on the bar," he confessed.

"How convenient? You left yo shit downstairs so you can fuck that bitch up here without distractions," she yelled.

"Mannnnn… Micah look, I told you what it was. I ain't gotta lie to you about shit. If I wanted to fuck the bitch, why fuck her in my office? Motherfucker you got a key…. How stupid do I look?" he shot back.

Micah stood there for a moment in silence before walking around him and grabbing her purse. Malik reached out and grabbed her arm before she could make it back to the door.

"You serious right now?" he asked.

"Let me the fuck go!" she mumbled before snatching away and walking downstairs.

Malik followed closely behind her but decided not to chase after her. He had done nothing wrong, and this was the first time their relationship was being tested. Not only was he telling the truth, but his head was banging. He didn't have the strength to deal with Micah's insecure bullshit right then.

When Micah left, Malik went to the bar to grab his phone. He had several missed calls from Micah and one from Goo. He dialed Goo back immediately, just in case he was already at his crib waiting on him.

"Nigga where the fuck you at?" Goo roared into the phone.

"My bad man.... I'm on my way now. Jayda ass popped up trying to seduce a nigga in his office then Micah walked in, snapping. Nigga it's all bad," Malik explained.

Goo started laughing hysterically which only pissed Malik off more.

"You done?" Malik asked, once Goo's laughter slowed down.

"My bad. I just think the shit funny, but you still got it good compared to me," Goo stated.

"What you talking about?" Malik inquired.

"Mannnnn... I just had to arrange a sit down with my baby momma and my wife."

"Get the fuck outta here. How you gon' pull that off?" Malik asked, walking to his car.

"Shiddddd... I have no idea. I texted Candy and asked her, she said ok, just let her know the time and place. I still ain't told her Mona pregnant. And then I ain't found out when Imma kill her new boyfriend yet either. Bruh, these hoes stressing me out," Goo admitted.

"Shit, tell me about it but I'm on my way. Be there in fifteen minutes," he said, ending the call and hopping on 290.

Chapter 17

Micah heard Malik as he followed behind her, but she didn't have time for his bullshit at the moment. Deep down, she figured that he was telling the truth about the Jayda bitch, but seeing her so close to Malik just pissed Micah the fuck off. After she hopped in her car, Micah's mind went back to the New Year's party that Malik had, and she was pretty sure that was the same chick that was escorted out.

"He gon' make me fuck him up for real" Micah mumbled to herself as she took off and headed towards Hyde Park to her parent's house. Her mom had texted the whole family that morning and told them that she was cooking and that she had some important news to share with them. Micah didn't have a clue as to what the news was, but when her mom said that she was making strawberry cheesecake, she was sold. Her mom made the best, and Micah would argue with anyone who disagreed. The way she put whipped cream on top was to die for. The ringing of Micah's phone broke her from her thoughts.

"Hey Candy!" Micah answered once the call connected to her Bluetooth.

"Hey girl… what you got going on?" Candy quizzed.

"Girl… I just left Malik's ass. I walked in on some bitch standing between his legs. He claim it was an old friend or whatever and she just so happen to drop by. The bitch left before I had to act a fool, but I'm not letting his ass off the hook that easy," Micah vented.

"What the hell? What's wrong wit' these niggaz? Malik shouldn't have let the bitch get close enough to be in an uncomfortable position, but I doubt he did anything. Although Goo gets on my fuckin' nerves at times, I will say that he's always honest, and I get the same vibe from Malik," Candy told her girl.

Micah sighed after she listened to Candy talk. It only confirmed what she felt. At that moment, she knew that she had to make it right with her man. Petty problems could lead to big problems, and they had been pretty solid so far. Micah didn't want to be the cause of them drifting apart. She made a mental note to text Malik once she arrived to her destination.

"You're right girl… thanks for making me realize it. You always know just what to say," Micah sincerely told her friend.

"That's what friends are for. You know I ain't one of them chicks that'll tell you what you want to hear, Imma keep it one hundred all the time," Candy admitted.

"I already know," Micah agreed,

"But anyways, what's been going on wit' you?" Micah continued.

"Girl… Goo wants to have a sit down with me, him, and Mona. I agreed to it, but I really don't know what to expect. I do know that I'll never let my baby go around that bitch until I talk to her face to face, so Imma go through with it," Candy clarified.

"I don't blame you on that… ohhh shit, speaking of Mona, did Goo tell you that bitch pregnant?" Micah quizzed.

"Hell naw his ass didn't… I guess he was gonna break that news during the come to Jesus meeting, but good looking out," Candy expressed.

They talked for a few more minutes and Micah listened as Candy gave her updates on RJ. Micah couldn't wait to go and see him again. She also listened as Candy talked about Trey. Micah knew that her girl was only using him as a distraction to keep her mind off of Goo, and she told her just that. She also warned her about playing any type of games because they both knew that Goo was a loose cannon. Once she pulled in her parent's driveway, she parked and texted Malik, who in return hit her right back.

Micah: I'll be by your house when I leave my parent's.

Malik: Bet.

Micah walked in and the smell of food made her stomach growl instantly. It was then that she realized that she hadn't eaten anything since she had a bowl of Cinnamon Toast Crunch earlier that morning. A home cooked meal was definitely needed, but Micah just couldn't fight off the nagging feeling that was in the pit of her stomach. She didn't know if it stemmed from Malik, or if was just the curiosity of not knowing what her mom wanted.

"Moommm," Micah squealed as she walked inside.

"I'm in the kitchen darling," her mom called out to her, and Micah headed that way.

"What's going on?" she queried.

"I'm going to tell you all at one time," her mom told her with a smile on her face that didn't quite reach her eyes.

So many thoughts had taken over Micah's mind. She wondered if her mom had found out about Mark and something had happened to him for real. As soon as that thought entered her mind, she dismissed it because Malik would have informed her. Micah thought about her dad and his suspicious behaviors and told herself that had to be the reason for the impromptu dinner and meeting.

"Are you and dad about to divorce?" Micah wondered.

"Huh? Where'd you get that from? Honey, stop trying to figure anything out and just relax. Your dad and sister should be walking in at any minute now," Mrs. Sanders noted.

It seemed as if her mom had a sixth sense or something, because as soon as the words left her lips, in walked Mesha and her dad. The expressions on their faces matched Micah's, and she knew that they were just as clueless as she was. Micah walked to the table and sat down. Her mom already had some of the food on the table, so she knew that it wouldn't be long before they would be eating.

"Hey Mesh, how's it going?" Micah spoke to her sister.

"It's been a day… didn't you make copies of everything when you did the books?" Mesha asked.

"Of course… they should be in the…" Micah started replying, but her dad cut her off.

"Mesha did you check your email? I sent you the copies that I had backed up because I moved some stuff to storage," Mr. Sanders stated.

Her dad's statement only confirmed that he was tied into some bullshit. Micah wanted to give him the benefit of the doubt, but he knew just as well as she did that Mesha never checked her email. It was just one of those things that she refused to do no matter how many times you told her. Mesha was a great worker, and she worked hard, but she didn't like technology. She didn't even have a Facebook account. Mesha had been hands on all her life, and everyone knew it.

"I didn't, but we still need the hard copies nearby. I'll need access because some things are off," Mesha replied.

"My lovely family!! I'm so happy to have everyone here," Mrs. Sanders said and then gave everyone a hug and a kiss before she took her seat.

"I wish Mark was here," Micah said and then she locked eyes with her dad.

"So do I baby… so do I," her mom said and sighed, and Mesha cosigned.

"Well, let's eat," her mom continued, and they all fixed their plates.

She had outdone herself, and it seemed as if she cooked some of everyone's favorite foods. Micah and Mark were both suckers for fried chicken, Mesha loved pork chops, their dad loved roast, and Mrs. Sanders was a fan of salmon. For her to cook some of all of it, Micah began to worry again. Mesha must have been reading her mind, because she beat Micah to asking the question that went unanswered earlier.

'Mom… what's going on? I mean, I know we all appreciate it, but what's really going on?" Mesha inquired.

"I want you all to enjoy your meals, and then I'll tell you all," Mrs. Sanders said and Micah detected sadness in her voice.

"Are you okay?" Michael asked his wife, and she simply nodded her head yes.

Everyone ate in silence for what seemed like an eternity, but in reality, only about five minutes has passed. The room was quiet and Micah could have sworn she heard the thoughts that were in everyone's heads.

"I have stage four breast cancer. I've done several different treatments, including ones that didn't make my hair fall out to keep anyone from knowing, but now it has spread to more areas of my body, and the doctors told me that I have less than three months to live. This is something that I've been battling for the past six months, and I'm at peace with it. Now, I want all of you to be at peace with it as well," Michelle finally spoke and broke the awkward silence.

Micah's mouth flew open to reply, but no words came out. Out of the corner of her eyes, she saw that her dad and sister were just as shocked as she was. Micah felt like the air had been sucked out of her. Although she heard every word that her mom had iterated, she just couldn't process it.

"What did you just say mom?" Micah inquired after several moments of dead silence.

"I know this is going to be hard, but we will get through it. We have no control over our time here on this earth, and unfortunately, my time is almost up. I need all of you to be strong," Michelle said, and Mesha broke down crying.

Once Micah looked around the room, she noticed that her dad already had tears streaming down his face. She had never seen her dad cry a day in his life, so she knew that the pain ran deep. Micah felt numb. She didn't know what else to say or do. Everyone except Micah got up and embraced her mom, and tears and sniffles filled the room. Micah told herself that she had to be the strong one. Someone had to take on the role, so it had to be her. She slowly got up and made her way towards her mom. Micah blinked several times in an attempt to hold her tears in. She couldn't let them fall.

"Mom… we're gonna get through this. I'm gonna find you the best doctor in the Midwest, and everything will be fine," she spoke once she got close to her mom.

Micah watched her mom as she gently pushed her dad and sister away, and then pulled her in for a hug. Still wanting and needing to be strong, Micah kept herself together.

"I'm gonna be strong for you mom. I love you," Micah said as she squeezed her mom tight.

"I love you too, baby," Michelle told her daughter.

"We need Mark here right now. We're incomplete… and I'm gonna get him," Micah said before she could stop herself.

"Sweetheart, I really wish you could get him… but we're gonna make it, okay. I admire you for being strong," Michelle told her daughter and then she backed up.

"I don't want a pity party around here. Things are gonna be just like normal," Michelle said and looked everyone in the eyes.

"Normal… how do you expect everything to be normal when you just told us that you're dying? How could you keep this kinda secret away from me?" Michael said in a voice mixed with sadness and anger.

"Like you're not keeping secrets yourself!" Micah exclaimed loudly.

"What's going on?" Mesha inquired as she wiped her face with the back of her right hand.

"I know that this was all a shock to everyone, but we aren't about to fall apart. Micah, I thought your dad was cheating on me at one time too, but he's not. And honey, I kept this to myself because I didn't want any pity. It was a decision that I made, and I don't regret it," Michelle addressed them.

"When is your next appointment?" Mesha quizzed.

"I'm not going to anymore appointments. There's no use, and I'm not going to continue putting my body through that turmoil," Michelle admitted.

Micah felt like she was about to lose it, so she grabbed her keys and phone and headed towards the door. She heard her dad and sister as they called out to her, but she ignored them. Micah also heard her mom telling them to give her some time, but she needed more than time. She thought about the strained relationship that she had with her mom growing up and how it had gotten better over the past few months. Once she made it outside, she dialed Malik's number, and as soon as he answered, Micah fell to ground and all of the emotions that she had been holding in poured out like a flood.

Chapter 18

Goo slammed the doors on his truck and power walked into the Marathon gas station on Independence. He was high and had the munchies like a motherfucker, so he went inside and grabbed two bags of Flamin' Hots, a Peach Lemonade Arizona, and a Twix. He opened the chips while standing in line waiting to pay. A group of chicks walked in laughing, all three of them eyeing him while he paid for his shit. Goo chopped it up with the owner of the gas station for a few seconds before he dipped out.

Once he made it outside, he threw the empty bag of chips on the ground and proceeded to open the other bag when he heard some noise behind him, which made him turn around.

"Why are you soooo fine?" the boldest one out of the three friends asked.

Goo cracked a smile before unlocking his Porsche Cayenne with the remote, when the same girl spoke up again.

"So you just gon' ignore me like that?" she asked.

Goo stopped walking and motioned with his hand for the girl with the big mouth to come over to where he stood.

"You know coming at niggaz is unattractive sweetheart," Goo schooled her.

The young girl's facial expression changed instantly, her pretty light skin was now fire red. She glanced back at her crew and then focused her attention back on Goo.

"My personality is not what I'm trying to make you attracted to," she replied with sass.

Goo couldn't help but laugh, he liked her feistiness.

"How old are you shorty?" he inquired.

"I'm twenty-one," she answered.

"Twenty-one, that means you really like nineteen," he corrected her.

The young chick rolled her eyes and blew her breath.

"Look, I think you fine and all and had this been like last year or some shit, I would have been fucking you later tonight. But you see, I got a wife that'll have her cousins beat yo ass and baby momma who would get both of our ass locked up," he chuckled.

Goo walked off and got into his car before she could reply. Truth was, shorty was fine and thick as fuck, but the last thing he needed right now was some more bullshit involving women. Especially since he was on his way to have a sit down with his wife and the woman he actually wanted to be with. Ever since finding out about Candy having a man, Goo had been in his feelings. He still was active in his son's life, but he wasn't really vibing with Candy how he used to. He used to chill with her and watch movies and shit while their son slept, but now he was in and out. His feelings toward the situation were crazy. He was really thinking about getting rid of Trey's ass, but how could he be that selfish when he had a whole wife at home.

"Speaking of the devil," Goo said aloud as an incoming call came from Mona.

"Yeah man!" he answered, through the speakers.

"What you mean…yeah man?" she asked with an attitude.

Goo shook his head while making a sharp right onto 16th and Trumbull.

"What's up Mona?" Goo inquired.

"I'm waiting on you. I thought we agreed to meet your little side bitch today," she replied.

"Look, all that side bitch shit ain't gon' fly at that meeting, so be cool," he snapped.

"Are you checking me for that bitch?" Mona yelled, her voice echoing through his truck.

"I ain't taking up for nobody. I'm just telling you to go into this shit with a respectable mind frame. I wouldn't let her disrespect you and I'm not....."

"YOU NOT WHAT? You keep forgetting that I am your wife, and she and I are not on the same level Rico," she said, cutting him off.

One minute, Mona was cool and the next she was always snapping about some shit. Goo let the majority of the shit slide because he knew her hormones were all out of whack, but he was getting fed up with her fat ass.

"Look man, meet me at Douglas Park. I'm on my way there now," Goo informed her.

"MEET YOU? We are supposed to come together Rico.... How would it look if we didn't arrive in the same car? It's bad enough you let her come in between us. She's really going to think we are divided if we show up in separate cars," Mona whined.

Goo banged his hands on the steering wheel before speaking.

"That's yo fuckin' problem! You always care about what the next motherfucker thinks. I'm tired of reminding you that you are my wife and my wife for a reason Mona. Pulling up in the same car ain't gon' change shit, and besides, I'm already out West and you at your mom's house, which is around the corner. Just meet me there NOW. Bye!" Goo yelled, ending the call before she could respond.

Before throwing his phone back in the cup holder, Goo noticed he had a text message from Candy.

Candy: We pulling up

Goo: Cool.... Me too

Goo slid through a few of his blocks, just to see if everything looked good before heading to the park. Although it was September, the temperature was still in the low 80's. Goo figured that meeting at a park was mutual grounds and everyone should be comfortable there. He pulled up beside Candy's candy apple red Mercedes Benz, said a silent prayer, and jumped out. He had no idea how this was going to go, but he prayed to the ratchet gods that everything would go smoothly.

"Hey baby daddy!" Candy said with a smile as Goo walked over to her car to help her with RJ.

"Attorney Williams," he greeted her back with a head nod.

"Oh my God, we are so formal today. Is that because wifey will be present?" she laughed.

"Shut up. You look nice though," he replied and ignored her comment about Mona.

"Thank you and try not to wake him up," she smiled and closed her car door.

Goo couldn't help but notice how beautiful Candy looked. She was rocking a pair of ripped up jeans that showed off her thick thighs and a white wife-beater with a tan leather jacket that matched the wheat Manolo Blahnik Timbs she was sporting.

"Let's sit over there. Out of the sun," Goo instructed and pointed to a nearby bench.

Goo and RJ walked off first, with Candy in tow.

"Great minds think alike, huh Goo?" Candy said out of the blue.

"What you are talking about girl?" he asked and then took a seat.

"You wanna be like me so bad," she stated, smiling.

It was then that Goo noticed that they were in fact dressed alike. Goo too sported a pair of raggedy jeans, a white Ralph Lauren Polo shirt and a pair of wheat Timberland boots, minus the high heel

123

like Candy's. It was crazy to him how in sync they were without even trying. He had to find a way to get that nigga Trey out of the picture and he knew just how.

"Man... he getting big!" Goo said and pulled the thin blanket from off his son.

"Yeah, he eats like you," Candy replied while looking in her phone.

Goo chuckled.

"Nah... not yet. He ain't eating like me until he at least eighteen."

Candy looked up from her phone and looked at Goo before playfully punching him in the arm.

"Stop being nasty," she giggled.

"I'm just saying," Goo replied.

"Ummmmm... hello!"

Both Candy and Goo looked up and out the corner of their eyes saw Mona standing there in a yellow maternity shirt with a pair of jeans to match and a pair of red Christian Louboutin pumps, rubbing her stomach.

"What up? Sit down," Goo said and scooted over to the side, so she could take a seat by him.

Mona screwed up her face at the both of them before popping a squat. The entire park was silent. It's like even the birds stopped chirping and that only made the shit more awkward.

"Soooooo....." Candy said, speaking up first, breaking the silence.

"Yeah, let's get this shit over with," Goo followed behind her.

"I know I'm the one who is responsible for this bullshit amongst y'all. And I've been apologizing since shit hit the fan, but the truth is, we all gotta co-exist. Candy, as you can see Mona's pregnant...."

"Congratulations!" Candy said, interrupting him.

Goo looked over at her and smiled, causing her to smile back. He loved her personality, she was so fuckin' dope. He never told her about Mona being pregnant, but here she was handling it like a champ, not letting the shit faze her.

"Un huh.... Thanks," Mona replied dryly.

"Like I was saying, y'all motherfuckers gotta get along, at least for my kids. I want JR and my other son to be in each other's lives," he paused.

"Awwww... RJ will have a little brother, what y'all naming him?" Candy leaned forward, directing her question at Mona.

Mona rolled her eyes and by the chuckle Candy let out, Goo knew she caught it.

"We haven't decided on a name yet, but I guess WE can't make him a junior, now can WE?" Mona smirked.

"Well, you can make him whatever the fuck you wanna make him," Candy snapped back.

"Aye aye aye.... Y'all cool out. Y'all waking up my son," Goo interjected, standing to his feet, rocking RJ back and forth.

The park was quiet again and everyone just looked around weirdly.

"Can I see him?" Mona asked as she stood to her feet.

Goo cut his eyes at Candy for her approval, but she only shrugged her shoulders. Once Mona got close enough, Goo handed RJ to Mona and she started smiling.

"He's so handsome. I can't wait to meet our baby," she cooed, while handing RJ back to Goo.

Goo was scared as fuck because that could have went way left because he knew how Mona really felt because all she did was express her feelings.

Goo sat back down with a now wide-awoke RJ and began to play with him, bouncing him up and down on his lap.

"You better stop. He just ate. He gon' throw up on yo ass," Candy said, searching through her Gucci diaper bag for a bib.

"Nah, my mans wouldn't do me like that. We got an understanding," Goo boasted.

Before he could complete his sentence fully, RJ exploded all over himself and Goo. Candy looked along and laughed hysterically. Goo joined in on the laughter as he snatched the bib from Candy and wiped the both of them off.

"Give me my baby," Candy said through laughter as she grabbed RJ from Goo.

"Mommy baby, why you do daddy like that, huh?" Candy said to her cheerful son.

"Yeah this nigga got me. Aye remember when we were in Punta Cuna and you threw up on me?" Goo reminisced.

"Stop bringing that up! I was pregnant nigga, and I couldn't hold it in," she replied.

"DAMN! Y'ALL WANT ME TO LEAVE Y'ALL ALONE!?" Mona yelled and stood to her feet.

Candy and Goo both forgot that Mona was even there, and the expressions on their face told it.

"Oh shit, my bad Mona," Goo apologized and stood up with her.

"Nah it's cool Goo. I see what it is," Mona said with tears in her eyes.

"What you mean by that?" Goo asked.

"This sit down was pointless. We got nowhere, but from this day out, I'll be cordial. Candy, I have nothing against you. You were just a random ratchet thot who ended up pregnant by my husband. Goo, you better hope this broke bitch don't put you on child support. I know a come-up queen when I see one," Mona ranted.

Both Candy and Goo's face screwed up at the same time. Candy stood to her feet with her son on her hip.

"You might wanna hold OUR child," Candy said and handed RJ off to Goo.

"Look bitch, I know your emotions are all over the place. I know I was just pregnant by YOUR husband not too long ago...remember, but I'm not finna let you keep taking jabs at me. Come- up? Bitch, I make well over two-hundred-thousand a year. That places me in a tax bracket of my own, so all that ratchet thot shit is falsified. I'm here because I was asked to come and truthfully, I'm not thinking about you or your husband. This baby mamma drama bullshit is so beneath me," Candy snapped, before snatching RJ out of Goo's arms.

Candy grabbed the diaper bag off the bench and walked off towards her car.

"Bae wait!" Goo yelled out to her and immediately regretted it.

"Bae?" Mona said in a low tone, but loud enough for Goo to hear.

Candy stopped and stood there, waiting to see what was next. She too was surprised that he addressed her in that way in front of Mona. Goo spent many nights telling Candy how much he loved her and wish she was the one he had married instead, but now was the moment of truth. Goo looked back and forth between the two women

127

confused. He was tired of playing the game and truthfully, a nigga was getting too old for it. The drama and trying to keep the both of them happy was too much for him.

"Tell that bitch she can go Rico!" Mona ordered.

Goo looked at his wife of almost four years and shook his head.

"Mona, I can't. I love you, but I haven't been in love with you for a while now. Candy got my heart. I just can't do this no more," Goo truthfully admitted before walking off to an awaiting Candy.

Goo took a few steps forward before turning around. Mona stood there with tears streaming down her face. He knew that he had hurt her with that confession, but it was long overdue. He was only married to her at this point because it was convenient, but Goo felt like he had to do what was right in his in heart…finally.

"FUCK YOU GOO! YOU! YO BITCH AND THAT BABY! YOU GON' REAP WHAT YOU SOW. WATCH YOU REGRET THIS SHIT!" Mona yelled out threats that didn't faze Goo, instead of reacting, he kept walking hand and hand with Candy.

Chapter 19

It took a whole week to convince Michelle to go to the appointment that she scheduled for her, but Micah wouldn't ease up until she gave in. The day that her mother told the family that she was dying, Micah held it together in front of everyone, but she lost it as soon as she made it outside and called Malik. Everyone in the house must have been in their own worlds, because no one knew that Malik had come by and picked Micah up until two days later, when she returned for her car. He left Goo and came to her rescue, despite the disagreement they had earlier that day, and Micah appreciated him for it.

Over the past week, Micah found herself researching the best doctors in the state, information on breast cancer, medications and treatments, and anything that she could think of that might be a help to her mom. She knew that her mom said there was nothing else that could be done, but Micah just couldn't settle for her words alone. She felt like she had to put forth effort to see if there were any other options. Micah told herself daily that there had to be some hope. The entire family was going to the appointment that Micah scheduled with Dr. Whitaker. They had two hours before it was time to arrive, so Micah was sitting in the living room at her parent's house, staring at the TV. She wasn't watching it, it was more like the TV was watching her.

"Can I talk to you for a minute, sweetheart?" Micah heard her dad asking from behind the chair that she was sitting in.

"Sure... talk," Micah dryly replied.

Micah didn't mean to disrespect her dad in any type of way, but she still felt some type of way about him, and it ate her up that she couldn't figure out what all he had going on. The bodies that were dropped off at the back of the funeral home, the books being off and missing, and his awkward behavior at times, and a few other details that Micah noticed had her mind on one hundred.

"Let's step outside," Mr. Sanders stated, and Micah slowly got up and followed behind him.

Micah watched her dad as he rubbed his temples with his eyes closed. He had lines in his forehead, and it appeared that he had aged ten years in just one week. She knew that the illness of her mom, on top of whatever else that he had going on, had to be stressing him out to the max.

"What all do you know?" her dad asked after several moments of silence.

"Know about what?" Micah inquired. She knew what he was talking about, but she knew what Mark and Malik told her, so she couldn't speak on it.

"You're a smart girl... Mikey, so what all do you know?" he father asked again as he called her by the nickname that was designated for Mark only.

"I know that you're hiding something, dad. I saw some of the books before you moved them, and remember I saw those bodies too. I wish I knew everything so that I could help you out of your mess, but I'm clueless. So, dad, what's really going on?" Micah shifted the conversation.

Her dad sighed and Micah wondered if he was about to let her know what the real deal was. She was tired of trying to guess and figure shit out, because several "off the wall" scenarios that she didn't even care to repeat had popped into her head.

"Everything is gonna be okay. If I could, I would explain it, but I really can't right now," her dad said after a few moments of silence.

"I guess we both have some secrets then... but just know that if this appointment doesn't go how I want it to go, my secret will be exposed and shortly after, yours will too," Micah said and walked back into the house.

When Micah made it to the living room, she saw her mom walking out of her bedroom. Micah could tell that her mom was tired by the look in her eyes, but she pushed through.

"You ready mom?" Micah inquired and as soon as she said it, Mesha walked out.

"I'm ready... I'm only doing this for you sweetheart, but please don't get your hopes up. I already know what's going to happen," Mrs. Sanders told her daughter.

"Stay positive, mom," Mesha chimed in.

"Right, please stay positive," Micah added.

They all gathered themselves and left about five minutes later. It was the first trip that they had made as a family in a long time, and the fact that it wasn't a pleasant trip had Micah deeper in her feelings. Micah sat in the backseat with Mesha while their dad drove them to the clinic. Facebook, Instagram, and Snap Chat were distractions that Micah took advantage of while on the way. She checked all of Tasha's sites, and she still didn't see any activity. Micah was beginning to think more and more that Tasha was just on some bullshit. After finding out about her mom though, she pushed all of that shit out of her head and focused on what was important.

Thirty minutes later, they were all sitting in a private room listening as the doctor spoke and read off Mrs. Sanders previous doctor's reports. Dr. Whitaker explained to them that if what he was looking at was accurate, then there wouldn't be much that anyone could do besides trying their best to keep the patient comfortable. When he was finished explaining everything, Dr. Whitaker had his nurse to take Michelle to the back to run some tests. Micah's stomach felt like it was in a million knots. She locked eyes and smiled at her mom before she left the room. Micah constantly told herself that she had to be the strong one and that was what kept her going. When she made the appointment, Micah listed her phone number as the contact for everything because she needed to know everything firsthand. Dr. Whitaker planned to read the results expeditiously.

An hour and a half later, Micah pulled into Candy's complex and sent her a text letting her know that she was outside. The testing didn't last long at all. Michael wanted to take the family out to eat, but Michelle was tired and requested to go home and lay down. Once Micah saw that she was resting, she kissed her and left out. She had so much that she needed to catch Candy up on. It seemed as if they hadn't talked in forever. Micah got out and walked up to the door and knocked.

"Hey boo," Candy spoke as soon as she opened the door holding RJ.

"Hey girl!" Micah replied and took RJ out of Candy's arms.

"He's getting sooo big… looking like his damn daddy," Micah continued as she smiled at RJ and played with him.

"He damn sure looks just like his ass," Candy sighed as she took a seat across from Micah.

"What's been goin' on?" Micah inquired.

"Giirrllll… let me tell you all about that so called sit down," Candy started, and Micah was all ears as she bounced RJ and kept him giggling.

Micah listened as Candy ran down every detail of the sit down to her. She laughed when her girl told her how she finally put Mona in her place after letting so much shade fly by. The shocker was when she listened to how Goo left Mona standing there crying and told her that he wanted to be with Candy. Micah's mouth flew wide open. She had to admit that her biggest issue with Goo was how he played both women when in her eyes, Candy was the better pick. It was true that Mona had sat through dinner with her and told her so much, but Micah was only being cordial. Candy was her girl and nothing could change that. She had to admit that she was happy to hear that Goo was ready to stop playing games.

"But what about Trey?" Candy said out of the blue and broke Micah out of her thoughts.

"What about him? You wouldn't choose Trey over Goo! Would you?" Micah quizzed with her head cocked to the side.

Instead of Candy responding, she got up and took RJ from Micah since he had fallen asleep, and Micah sat there as she walked towards the back. When she returned to the living room, Candy sat in the spot that she had previously occupied, and Micah gave her a knowing look that said "spill it."

"I love Goo… you know this, but I just have to make sure that he is serious before I cut ties with Trey. What if he goes back to Mona?" Candy asked.

"That is something to think about, but don't just string that man alone if you know you aren't feeling him," Micah said and then her phone rang with a number she didn't recognize.

"Hello," Micah answered after a few seconds.

The nervousness that she had possessed for the last week kicked back in when she heard Dr. Whitaker's voice on the other end of the phone. She knew that he was going to get the results fast, but she had no idea that it was going to be the same day. Micah listened to him, and she didn't even realize that she was crying until Candy grabbed the Kleenex from the table and wiped her tears for her. When she finally hung up, Micah sat there in silence for what seemed like an eternity.

"I know I'm not supposed to, but I gotta call my brother. I can't let my mom die without him having the chance to see her," Micah sobbed and Candy hugged her tighter.

Chapter 20

Malik grabbed the yellow tulips off the passenger's side seat of his two-door Camaro and exited the vehicle. It was early October and the scenery looked as such. The breeze was crisp and the multi-colored leaves crunched under his Timbs as he made his way through Oak Lawn cemetery. He walked a few more minutes before he came to a stop. He glanced down at the heart-shaped tombstone and smiled as he read the inscription.

In Loving Memory of

Mary L. Jefferson

Sunrise May 1, 1955 - Sunset November 4, 2007

"Love is holding on to memories that only the heart can see!"

It had been a while since Malik visited his mother's grave, not because he had forgotten about her, but because it was still all too painful. As he stared at the tombstone, he saw that in a few weeks, it would be exactly ten years that his angel had been watching over him. When Micah came to him and revealed the news about her mother, it hit Malik harder than he could have imagined. His mother also was a victim of breast cancer, so he knew exactly what his girl was going through. Malik vowed to be there for Micah each step of the way. Micah told him that her and her mom never had a close relationship as she grew up, but at the end of the day, she still birthed her and to watch her die was heartbreaking.

Malik spent about twenty minutes talking to his mother, filling her in on everything that was going on in his life. He made sure to tell her about how much he loved Micah and wished she was here to meet her. Malik knew his mother would love his woman, she would have admired Micha's hustle and drive, and that was the exact reason Malik had finally made up his mind. He was going to make Micah his wife. Malik said his final goodbyes to his mother and made his way back to his car. Once inside, he shot Goo a text message.

Malik: What you on nigga?

Goo: At Candy's crib. Waddup

Malik: I'm finna slide thru, I gotta holla at you about some shit

Goo: Bet

Malik tossed his phone on the passenger's seat and headed towards Candy's house. Traffic was surprisingly light, so he made it there in record time; a little under fifteen minutes. He lucked up on a park right in front and hopped out. He skipped up the few stairs out front and rang the doorbell. A few seconds later, Candy opened the door.

"What's up baby momma?" Malik greeted her.

"What's up God Daddy?" she replied back and then opened the door wider, allowing him to enter.

Malik walked pass her and straight into the living room where Goo and RJ were located. RJ was sitting up with the help of his father, watching cartoons. He looked so in tune, like he knew what was going on. The sight of Goo and his junior caused Malik to smile. He couldn't wait until his turn; he wanted that bond more than anything.

"What's up my niggggaaaa!" Malik said, walking over to the couch, grabbing RJ and twirling him in the air.

RJ giggled uncontrollably as slob spilled from his teething gums. Once Malik began to feel himself getting dizzy, he stopped and took a seat on the cream leather loveseat with RJ on his lap.

"Nigga, I think you more into this shit then he is," Malik said to Goo who was focused on the TV.

Goo looked up briefly and stuck up his middle finger before turning his attention back to the television.

"Rugrats use to be my shit," he confessed.

"Yeah I see!" Malik said while he pulled his car keys from RJ's mouth.

The three of them sat there in silence and Malik found himself drawn to the Nickelodeon show as well.

"Malik, you hungry? I just made some tacos," Candy walked in the living room and asked.

"Nah I'm good. I just came over here to talk to y'all about something real quick," he replied.

"What's up?" Candy asked as she wiped her hands on a napkin.

Malik stood up and handed RJ back to Goo before sitting back down and speaking.

"Imma ask Micah to marry me!" he blurted out and both Candy and Goo's eyes popped out of their sockets.

"You what?" Goo yelled.

"Imma ask shorty to marry me," he restated, feeling more confident about his decision every time those words left his mouth.

"You sure?" Goo questioned, now giving his full attention to his right-hand man.

"Yeah I'm sure. I love the fuck out that girl, and I wanna keep it that way for the rest of my life," Malik admitted truthfully.

"Well nigga, you got my blessings. I know me and Micah has had our differences, but I've never seen you like this over a woman, except for...."

Goo stopped in mid-sentence when he saw the look on Malik's face.

"Never mind... but congratulations my dude," Goo finished and stood to his feet, and then walked over to Malik and pulled him up into a manly hug.

After their brief embrace, they both turned around and noticed Candy standing in the same spot.

"What the fuck you over there crying for?" Goo shouted out, which caused Malik to laugh.

"I'm just so happy. I love Micah like a sister, and I know how much she loves you Malik. I think y'all are perfect for each other," she sobbed.

Malik looked at Candy and shook his head, she was being so dramatic, but Malik could tell it was genuine. That was why he had to make her aware of something.

"Look Candy, you can not say one word to Micah. I want this to be a surprise; as a matter of fact, I wanna have an engagement party," Malik let it be known.

"Oh my God, I'm planning it. I was going to be a party planner had I not passed the bar. Malik just let me know how you want things; as a matter of fact, don't tell me shit. I'm going to do this how I want to. Micah's my girl, I know what she wants. I'll get back to you later this week with a date and venue, just to see if it works for you," Candy replied excitedly, before she turned and headed upstairs.

Malik and Goo both looked at each other and started laughing.

"I fucks with Candy man. I'm glad you left Mona ass alone. Speaking of her, what's been going on?" Malik inquired.

"Shit. I been calling her, and she ain't answer not one time. I went by the house and every time I stop by, she ain't there," Goo filled him in.

"Fuck you steady sliding over there for?" Malik quizzed.

"Nigga, by law, that's still my wife and she's still carrying my child. I kinda feel bad about it, but it had to be done," Goo responded.

"Yeah I hear you," Malik replied and stood to his feet.

Truthfully, he hated the fact that Goo married that bitch, but that was his business. Goo told Malik about Mona's final words before they left her at the park. Malik took that as a threat, and he promised to God that if Mona fucked with anything concerning their businesses, Malik would put a bullet in her head himself.

"Aight homie, I'm finna head out. I gotta go check on Micah."

"Aight big fella. Lock the door behind you," Goo said and took a bite out of one of the tacos on his plate.

Malik left and headed towards Micah's condo. He parked in one of the two spots that belong to her and got out. He made a mental note to holler at her about getting a new car. He was sick of that fucking Maxima. He went to the seventh floor and used his key to gain access. The house was quiet and everything was calm, just the way he liked it. He walked to the back of the house into Micah's bedroom. She was laid across the bed on the phone.

"What's up baby?" she turned around and greeted him.

"What up? Who you talking to?" he asked.

"Candy's crazy ass."

"Straight up, what she talking about?" Malik wondered.

"Nothing, she's in a good mood for some reason. I guess Goo just dicked her down," Micah assumed.

"Aw ok cool... but... ummmmm... tell her you will call her back so I can dick you down," Malik smiled while licking his lips.

Micah giggled like an innocent school girl.

"Girrrlll... let me call you back," she said and ended the call.

Malik laughed at her. Micah was always willing to please him whenever and wherever, and he loved that about her.

"How you want it?" Micah asked, bending over with her fat ass in the air.

"Just like that!" he cheesed and came up behind her and smacked her on her ass.

Just as Malik began to help Micah remove her panties, there was a knock on the door. The both of them let out a loud frustrated grunt.

"You expecting somebody?" Malik asked, playing with Micah's pussy.

"Noooooo," she whined.

"Well let's ignore them then," Malik replied.

"No baby. It may be Mesha. Give me a few seconds, I'll be right back," Micah said, fixing her clothes and grabbing her robe off the chaise and slipping it on.

"Aight hurry up!" Malik yelled out to her as she disappeared in the hallway.

Chapter 21

Johnathan's attempt to make Micah jealous hadn't quite worked out like he hoped it would. He had meticulously planned out everything from the time that she would walk out of Micro Economics class to each step that it would take him to be in her direct path. He simply used Karla as a pawn, but the shit still didn't work. Ever since the incident, Karla was pissed at him because she felt like he didn't defend her like she thought he should have. Johnathan had hopes that she would leave him alone since she fussed so much, but instead, she did the complete opposite. Karla was on him so bad that it got to the point where it almost fucked up what he had going on.

Micah's routine used to be easy for Johnathan to follow, but she had switched things up. The day of the incident on campus, he actually went to her parent's house in hopes that she would show up so that he could tell her everything Terrance said about Tasha's visit to him, but she never did show up. If his guess was correct, he knew that Micah saw his car and kept going because her normal routine had always been to go home on Tuesdays. John sat at his computer desk surfing the web. His eyes lit up in amazement when he saw the icon light up that Micah's car moved from its spot. He had slipped and put a tracker on it earlier that day while she was in class so that he could find out where she lived. Following her would eventually become risky, so Johnathan decided to just install the device on her car that he ordered online.

After sitting there and devising a solid plan, Johnathan searched for nearby florists and placed an order for two dozen roses of various colors. He smiled as he went to hop in the shower with high hopes that he was going to win Micah back over. All he needed was a few minutes for her to listen to him, and everything would be fine. If she was still being stubborn, John was ready and willing to take her out because he refused to live another day without her. The more he thought about it, he toyed around with the idea of killing Malik. Everything was perfectly fine in Johnathan's eyes until that Malik character came along. He washed himself thoroughly while in the shower, all while singing, smiling, and constantly thinking.

When John got out of the shower, he dried off and wrapped his towel around the lower portion of his body and then walked to his closet. Since Micah ditched him for a street dude, John had purchased a couple of new outfits. He got dressed in one of the exact same outfits that he saw Malik dressed in on one of the pictures that Micah had posted on her Facebook page. After checking himself out in the mirror, Johnathan thought he looked good in his all black Balmain attire. He reached under the bed and retrieved the black nine millimeter that he bought a few weeks back and placed it in his pocket.

"Please don't make me have to use this on you, Micah," Johnathan mumbled to himself.

He went back to his computer and checked the location of the car again. It was still parked at Michigan Avenue, so Johnathan pretty much confirmed that it had to be the address of Micah's new residence since the apartment she had once occupied with Tasha was now vacant. Just in case the car moved, he closed his laptop, put it in the bag, and carried it with him. Johnathan hopped into his blue Jeep Cherokee and made his way to the florist. Upon arrival, he had to wait about thirty minutes before his order was ready, but he didn't mind.

Once he was done, he plugged the address that was stored into his memory into the GPS and headed towards his destination. Johnathan said a silent prayer that Micah would be alone and that she would hear him out. He wasn't prepared to live another day without her, and he meant it. Johnathan pulled up to 122 Michigan Avenue twenty minutes later, and he spotted Micah's Maxima. He checked the surroundings and noticed that it was a very nice location. The Micah that he once knew didn't care about spending a lot of money on material stuff, so he knew that it had to be her new man that made her move to the current location. Johnathan shook his head in disgust and wished that he could run into Malik before he saw Micah.

After a few minutes of thinking, Johnathan grabbed the roses and got out of his car. He wasn't sure which condo Micah lived in, but judging by the location of her car, he only had a few to choose from. He took his chances by knocking on the door of the closest one first, but no answered. He tried again, but got the same results.

"Hopefully it'll be the next one. I don't need anyone calling the cops on me," he mumbled to himself, and then proceeded a few steps to the right.

Johnathan knocked, and just when he felt defeated and turned to leave, he heard the door crack open. He turned around and smiled into Micah's beautiful face, but the same gesture wasn't returned.

Chapter 22

"Whoever this is better want something very got damn important... fuckin' up my groove," Micah fussed as she went to her door.

Only a handful of people knew where she lived, and no one had called so she had no idea who was knocking. If she hadn't just hung up with Candy, Micah would have assumed it was her, but her ass was all giggly, and Micah was trying to be the same way. She didn't even bother to ask who it was because she had chunked it up to being her sister, but when she locked eyes with Johnathan, her mood instantly changed. There he stood, grinning like a Cheshire cat while holding an assortment of roses.

"What the fuck are you doing here? How did you even know where I live?" Micah spat.

"I put a trac... I mean I... I just found out, okay. But none of that matters. I just came to claim what's rightfully mine," Johnathan said as he walked closer to the door.

"What the fuck? Rightfully yours? Are you stuck on stupid or some shit? I... DO... NO... WANT... YOU!!" Micah emphasized with a clap between each word.

Micah knew that no one would tell him where she lived, but it sounded to her like he was about to say he put a tracker or some shit somewhere. She made a mental note to have Malik check her car.

"You'll always be mine," Johnathan said and snapped Micah from her thoughts.

"Johnathan, get away from here, okay!" Micah replied and tried to close the door, but John stopped her.

"What the fuck are you doing?" she fumed.

"I just wanna talk to you. We can do this the easy way or the hard way!" he told her with a voice laced with venom.

Micah pushed him, and the vase with the roses that he was holding fell to the ground and shattered. When he looked down, Micah used that moment to push him again, but Johnathan forcefully pushed his way into the house after he shoved Micah down.

"See what you made me do!" Johnathan screamed and tried to help her up.

"WHAT THE FUCK IS GOIN' ON?" Malik yelled when he rounded the corner.

"Is you outta yo fuckin' mind?" Malik continued as he walked up to Johnathan and grabbed him by the neck with his right hand only.

Micah stared at Johnathan, and she wanted to fuck him up herself, but she knew that Malik had everything under control. She saw Johnathan struggling to catch his breath, but Micah also noticed that he was trying to reach in his pocket to grab something. Malik must have noticed it too, because he dropped him to the floor and then reached into his pocket and pulled out a black nine.

"Damn... you were coming to kill me because I don't want you?" Micah assessed.

Johnathan laid on the floor gasping for air, and Malik had eyes full of rage because they had appeared to change color and size. Before anyone else could speak a word, Micah watched Johnathan's body as it slumped to the floor after Malik released a single shot to the dome. After being in the street game for a minute, Micah had known people who had gotten dealt with by any means necessary. However, it was the first time that she had ever been that close and personal to a murder, especially to someone she knew; but surprisingly, she didn't even flinch. She knew what type of man she dealt with, and all types of shit came along with the territory. If Malik had let anyone force their way into her place of peace without any consequences, Micah would have questioned him.

"I got some trash that needs disposing... yeah... 122 Michigan Ave... bet!" Micah heard Malik say into the phone.

"You good babe?" he asked her.

"I'm great!" she told him and smiled.

"I need to start back shooting... I haven't fired a gun since Mark..." Micah started saying and then cut her sentence off.

"I got you, but for now... let's get outta here. Take those clothes off and put 'em in a garbage bag. We can shower at my house. We gotta get outta here," Malik told her.

An hour and a half later, Malik had Micah pinned against the shower wall as he stroked her as she screamed out in pleasure and dug her nails into his back. She lost count on how many times she had already came, but it was somewhere between three and five. When they got in the shower fifteen minutes prior, they both had washed each other off two times each, and Micah had become horny as hell. Malik gave her exactly what she needed, and she couldn't be happier. Micah felt her legs as they began to shake uncontrollably. She felt like she was about to fall, but Malik held her up.

"I got you bae... let that shit go," he coaxed her.

"Shit... oh my gawwddd," Micah squealed.

A few minutes later, they both came simultaneously, washed off in lukewarm water, and threw on some lounging clothes. Micah snuggled up next to Malik in his California King bed, just enjoying the moment.

"What's on your mind?" Malik asked her.

"You think I should reach out to Mark?" she finally asked him after several moments of thinking.

"I said I was going to, but I couldn't do it until I saw how you felt about it," she continued.

"You should... we only get one mom, ya know... and he should be able to see her before... you know what I mean," Malik told her as he rubbed her back.

"That's what I was thinking… I just can't believe this shit is happening. I'm glad you give me the chance to be weak when I'm wit' you, because I feel like I gotta be strong for my dad and Mesh," Micah admitted.

"I got you baby… this shit won't be easy, but I'll be wit' you every step of the way," Malik told her and then kissed her forehead.

"I love you," Micah said.

"I love you too, babe," Malik replied and shortly after, Micah drifted off to sleep in his arms.

The next day, Micah went to class and knocked out a quiz. The air outside was crisp, but it felt good to her. As soon as Micah got in her car, she sighed and placed the phone call that had been on her mind. She didn't even know if Mark was going to answer, but it had to be done and Malik agreed. After five rings, the call connected, but all Micah could hear was breathing for a few moments.

"What's wrong?" Mark finally spoke.

"We need you," Micah replied as she choked back her tears.

She talked to her brother for a few more minutes, and he explained to her that he had to work some shit out and then he would find a way to dip in. Micah didn't go into detail about the life span that the doctors had given. She just had faith that her brother would show up within a few weeks before things took a turn for the worse. The truth of the matter was, none of them knew exactly how long Michelle would live, but that didn't stop them from praying for a turn around.

Micah sat in her car for what seemed like forever after she hung up the phone with her brother. She was just stunned at how life played out. Just when things were going so well, it seemed like everything took a turn for the worse. The stunt that Johnathan pulled weighed heavily on her mind. Her phone chimed and broke Micah from her thoughts.

Candy: What's up girl... just thought about you and wanted to check on you since you never called back last night.

Micah: Girl, I gotta fill you in on some shit. You free for lunch?

Candy: Yep... Imma run by the daycare and peek in on RJ and we can meet at Miller's on North Riverside in 45 minutes.

Micah: Okay!

Since Micah had a few minutes to spare, she clicked on Snapchat since it had been a long time since she had been on. As she scrolled through, she viewed stories of a few people and was about to log back off until she saw that Tasha had posted a snap the night before. When Micah clicked on it, the only thing it said was "New Beginnings Coming Soon" with some airplanes.

"So this bitch is alive and just ain't reached out. Malik was right!" Micah mumbled to herself as she shook her head and finally pulled off.

Chapter 23

Two Weeks Later

"Damn… you really pulled this shit off in two weeks. I'm impressed… and even though you saying no, I still gotta pay you," Malik said as he looked around the venue.

"If you don't shut up… Micah is my girl. I'm not charging you… I'm just glad you like it. Tonight is gon' be perfect," Candy said as she put last minute touches on the décor.

"You sure she don't know shit? How you gon' get her here?" Malik quizzed.

"Nope… she will be happy and surprised. I asked her to go with me to a gala for work and she accepted. I got this, Malik… where the ring at though?" Candy asked him.

Malik reached into his pocket and pulled out a black velvet box, and when he opened it, Candy's eyes bucked.

"Oh myyyy gawwdddd!!! That ring is EVERYTHING!!!" Candy approved.

"Ten carats… I hope she like it!" Malik expressed.

"Nigga! Are you crazy? Micah is going to loovvveeee that rock… you know she ain't hard to please," Candy pointed out.

"You right… that's one of the things I love about her," Malik confessed.

"Wait…. don't you start that crying shit," Malik said as he looked at Candy.

"Okay okay… I'm just so happy for y'all," Candy laughed.

"Aight, well I'm bout to dip out… and thanks again man… this shit is nice," Malik said and left.

Malik walked out the Venue Six10 pleased at what Candy had done. Shorty definitely had skills, and Malik was going to pay her one way or another; whether she wanted him to or not. Business was good, but it wouldn't be Malik if he didn't check on shit anyway. He knew that he needed to get a cut, but before going to the barbershop, he headed towards the club. If it was up to him, he would've had the party at the club, but Candy insisted that it was too cliché and that it will be like no thought was put into it. He was glad that she took over everything and made it happen.

Even though he wouldn't be at the club that night, Malik trusted his staff. It was a well-known fact that he didn't fuck around when it came down to business and everyone knew it, therefore, they always stayed on top of their shit. Malik updated the inventory list when he made it upstairs for the order that he would be placing the next week. The holiday season was quickly approaching, and he knew from experience to order in advance before the vendors jacked their prices up.

Once Malik was done at the club, he headed to the barber shop. When he arrived twenty minutes later, it was packed just as he expected it to be, but that wasn't a worry of his. As soon as Malik walked in, he saw a dude getting out of JB's chair, so he headed straight for it and sat down. Several people spoke to him and dapped him up, and Malik returned the favor as he walked across the floor towards the chair he had occupied for the past five years. Malik heard a grunt from some dude that was sitting there waiting, but he cut his eyes and ignored him because he knew that JB would handle it.

"This VIP status right here youngster, don't start no shit. I'll get you next," JB told the impatient guy, who didn't say another word.

"What's up nigga? I was looking for you to be here early this morning, but you know I got you," JB directed his attention to Malik.

"I had some shit to take care of," Malik said, as he thought about his trip to the jewelry store to pick up Micah's ring.

While JB cleaned the clippers, Malik slipped his hand in his pocket and pulled out the same box that he showed Candy that morning. He opened it when he saw that all eyes were on him.

"Yoooo... Malik you bout to get married nigga?" one of the guys who was sitting in Greg's chair asked.

"Look at that rock! Micah done pussy whipped this nigga good!" JB chimed in.

The entire barber shop erupted into laughter, including Malik.

"Congratulations man!" a few guys exclaimed.

"If I had me a dime like Miss Micah, I would settle down too, but for now... fuck it," a young cat named Benny said.

"When you popping the question?" JB asked, after all of the excitement and shit talking died down.

"Tonight... come through if you done here. I'll shoot you the address," Malik replied.

"I'll do that... you got a good one man. I didn't think I would ever see the day yo ass got put on lock again," JB chuckled.

"Neither did I, but I feel good about it," Malik replied.

He knew who JB was referring to, but he refused to entertain the thought. Everything in the past was just that, and Micah was his future. He couldn't wait to make her Micah Jefferson. While JB was hooking Malik up, Goo walked into the shop and dapped everybody up.

"I got next!" he said as he walked over to JB's station.

"I got you homie," JB replied.

The same young guy that talked shit under his breath earlier hopped up.

"I thought I was next!" he shouted.

Both Malik and Goo chuckled after JB gave him a look that made him sit the fuck down. No matter who was in the shop or how long they had been there, when Malik or Goo walked in, they were priority. JB was part of the team, in more ways than one. To keep shit smooth, they still paid and tipped him well. Most people knew not to put up a fuss, but every now and then, there was that one. An hour later, JB was done with Malik and ready to line Goo up. Malik told everyone he would holla at them later and left. He had a few more things to knock off of his list for the night, and then he could chill out until it was time to get dressed.

***

Since Micah's Friday's class was cancelled, she went home to spend some time with her mom. They ate breakfast, and even though Micah didn't care for soap operas, she laid in bed and watched "The Young and the Restless" with her mom. She recalled watching a few episodes as a child and remembered seeing Victor Newman.

"That man ain't dead yet?" Micah said when he appeared on the screen.

"If Victor dies, they might as well cancel the show," her mom chuckled.

Micah tried her best not to think about her mom's illness, but it was very hard not to. She always heard older people say that you shouldn't question God, but she questioned him daily. If he had all of the answers, she wondered what was so wrong with asking him questions.

"Do you believe in miracles?" Micah asked her mom when a commercial came on.

"Of course I do," her mom replied.

"Are you praying for one? Because that's what I've been doing. I don't ask God for much, so I figure he should give me this one," Micah uttered.

"Whatever is meant to be will be, sweetheart... and whatever happens, just know that I'm okay with it," Michelle replied.

Micah didn't like her answer, but she didn't want to upset her mom in any kind of way, so she left it alone. As soon as twelve o'clock hit, they both got up. Micah watched her mom as she walked into her closet. Before she could follow, her phone rang. She connected the FaceTime call from Candy before it went to voicemail.

"Hey Candy girl!" Micah greeted.

"Hey girl... are you ready to go pick out a dress? I saw one that will be so cute on you," Candy jested.

"Would you be mad if backed out? I know the gala is tonight, but I really just wanna spend some time with my mom," Micah sighed.

"You're gonna leave me stuck, but I do understand," Candy pouted.

"Micah don't cancel your plans for me... me and your dad are going out anyway," Michelle called out to her.

"Moms being nosey... I guess I won't back out. You heard her," Micah laughed.

"Well come on and meet me at the mall, so you can get this dress," Candy beamed.

"Okay. Let me tell finished up here, and I'll meet you there," Micah said, then she ended the call. Still not ready to depart ways with her mom, she hung out about another 15 minutes before she actually left. Micah made sure to hug and kiss her mom before she left for the mall.

An hour later, Micah turned into Oak Brook mall and parked at the Neiman Marcus entrance since Candy texted and told her to come there. Micah wasn't in a big shopping mood, so she hoped she liked the dress that Candy had been raving over so that she could be in and out. She grabbed her purse after parking and turning the car off, and then headed inside. Micah called Candy as she walked in, but hung up immediately because she spotted her upon entrance. Candy turned around and saw Micah, and she headed towards her. Micah stared at the dress that her friend was holding, and it was indeed stunning.

"Girrrlllll... that. Dress. Is. BAADDD!! You must think I'm going to try to snag me a lawyer," Micah laughed, as she emphasized each word.

"No silly... but it's a white and gold theme. I found a bad ass gold dress, and when I saw this one, I knew you would love it," Candy cackled.

"I do love it... let me go try it on," Micah said, as she got the dress from Candy.

She made her way to the dressing room and took her clothes off. Before she put the dress on, Micah searched for the price tag, but it wasn't on there. She noticed that it was a Tom Ford dress and was skeptical about trying it on.

"What the hell... we only live once," Micah mumbled as she pulled the dress over her head.

She stared at herself in the mirror and was in awe. The white Tom Ford Crepe dress was simple, but beautiful. It hugged Micah in all the right places. As Micah stared at herself in the three-way mirror admiring the dress, she couldn't help but to think about how she would much rather be wearing that dress somewhere with Malik instead of with a bunch of strangers.

"Girl come on out... I know you love it even more now that it's on," Candy called out to her.

Micah walked out of the dressing room, and Candy handed her a gold pair of Giuseppe Zanotti heels.

"Don't say a word, just put 'em on," Candy silenced her, and Micah followed her command.

"You look absolutely amazing," a cheerful worker came up and greeted.

"Don't she though… you like it Micah?" Candy quizzed.

"I do… but…" Micah started saying, but Candy cut her off.

"No buts… it's already paid for," Candy told her.

"What? Candy, I'm not letting you pay for this!" Micah called out to her.

"It's already done… now come on," Candy said from a distance.

Micah had known Candy long enough to know that once her mind was made up, it was just that, so she mentally surrendered. After Micah went and put her clothes back on, the same sales lady that complimented her was at the door waiting when she walked out of the dressing room.

"I'll bag these items up for you" she smiled.

"Thank you," Micah told her and made her way over to the jewelry where Candy was.

After they left Neiman Marcus, Candy convinced Micah to get her nails and feet done, and they also got their eyebrows threaded. Candy tried to pay, but Micah wasn't having it. She told her that she had done enough. Even though Micah wasn't working, she had a pretty nice stash as well as money in the bank. Malik always dropped her more money than she could spend, and she saved it. It was almost five o'clock by the time they finished with everything, which included Micah getting her hair straightened by Candy's beautician.

"Girl... I'm going to take a nap... I'm tired as hell. I hope all of this prepping and shit don't go in vain because I feel like I could go to sleep for the night," Micah fussed.

"I'll call and wake you up. It starts at seven, but we can get there like eight and make an entrance. I'll pick you up," Candy said as they parted ways.

Micah went through Cane's driveway and ordered a chicken strip meal and ate on the way home. Malik had given her the okay to go back to her Condo, but Micah was really a little scared. She had never knowingly slept anywhere that someone had been killed, and she honestly didn't know if she wanted to even try. Micah didn't want to seem ungrateful, but a part of her wanted to ask Malik if it was possible for her to change units. There was a vacant one in the next building, and in her mind, it shouldn't be a problem moving. Micah commanded Siri to call Malik, and he answered after the third ring.

"What's up babe?" he spoke.

"Candy got me tired as hell... I don't even know if Imma make it to this lil gala shit wit' her because she done wore me out... but the dress she found for me is sooo beautiful. She paid for it, but Imma pay her back because I know this cost a grip, along with the shoes and the necklace," Micah rambled.

"You gon' have to send me a pic, so I can see if it's okay to let you out looking so fly," Malik joked.

"About that... I think I wanna come to your crib to get dressed. I don't know about living where a dead body was," Micah fretted.

"I had a feeling you was gon' feel some type of way. Your man is two steps ahead of ya. Stop by the leasing office and get your new keys. Everything from your condo has been moved," he emphasized.

"Damn... you're the best baby," Micah cooed.

She talked to Malik for a few more minutes and then pulled up to the leasing office of Michigan Ave Condos twenty minutes later. Micah went inside, and as promised, they handed her new keys, and she went about her way. Her new spot was on the back side and even though the area was already nice and quiet, she felt like that location would be much better. Micah went inside, set her alarm, wrapped her hair, and then crawled under the covers, and was asleep within minutes.

***

Malik glanced at the time and noticed that it was already fifteen minutes after six. He had been ripping and running all day, and did something that he hadn't done since he was a kid when he made it to the crib; he took a damn nap. When Micah had called him earlier, he was out picking up his suit and shit. He was tempted to tell her to go on to his house, but in the back of his mind, he knew that they would've ended up fucking once he made it, and that would have thrown the timing off for everybody. Candy was on his ass about being on time. She told him that he had to be there on time because she was going to be late on purpose to pick Micah up. He had to admit, Candy had the shit planned to the tee.

Malik got dressed in his all white Tom Ford suit after he got out of the shower. It was something else that Candy picked out, and he loved it. He sprayed on Issey Miyake, grabbed his phone, keys, and the ring and headed out. When Malik hopped into his truck, it was two minutes until seven. He knew that Micah's parents were probably there, but he hoped there wouldn't be anyone else waiting. Malik sped the whole way, and fifteen minutes later, he turned into the parking lot and found a few other cars.

After he parked, he got out and went and unlocked the doors. When he saw Michael and Michelle, he waited on them. Malik had talked to both of them the week before and received their blessings. That made everything official to him. He ushered them inside and got the results that he had hoped for. Malik knew that if her mom loved the place, so would she. Everyone gathered in and began mingling right away. His guys went straight to the open bar, and the others that Micah's mom invited mostly went to fix plates. Candy told Malik that she would have Micah there by eight, so all he had to do was wait the next hour out.

Chapter 24

"Girrlll... Malik and Goo who?" Candy joked before they walked out of Micah's place.

"Aight... make Goo kick yo ass. He probably ready to kick Trey's already," Micah laughed.

"I'm sure... he'll be alright though," Candy replied.

"If this event is boring, we gon' have to go somewhere afterwards because we look too damn good to waste these outfits," Micah told her friend.

She hopped in the passenger seat and snapped pictures of the both of them as Candy drove. Micah made a Facebook status and tagged the location that they were heading to. She couldn't wait to arrive, so she could get someone to take full body pics of them, and she needed to send Malik one as well.

"Does your job have the event at this location every year?" Micah asked, as they pulled up.

"Ummm, they change venues every year. Honestly, this is my first time going to this particular one. I wanna see what all the hype is," Candy replied as she found a parking spot right at the door.

"You VIP?" Micah quizzed.

"Something like that," Candy replied and winked.

"Come on... let's go crank this shit up," Candy said as she opened the door.

Micah followed suit. Candy stared at her phone, and Micah wanted to ask her what was wrong, but before she could, Candy started back walking.

"You go in first... I'm tryna see if Goo bout to call. He just texted me," Candy said.

"Girl, if you don't bring yo ass on. You drug me to this remember," Micah fussed, but she went ahead and opened the door.

"SURPRISE!!!!!!" everyone screamed as soon as she walked in.

"Oh my God!!! What's going on?" Micah asked everyone, but no one in particular.

She gazed around the room, and it was occupied with maybe twenty to thirty people who were all related or close friends of either her or Malik. Micah spotted her mom, dad, Mesha, Goo, a few people from church, and some of Malik's friends that she met before. She took in the beautiful gold and white decorations, and when she saw the picture that her and Malik had taken in Punta Cuna blown up, she almost cried. Just as Micah was about to ask where Malik was, "Lifetime" by Prophet Jones started playing and the lights dimmed.

♫*"I been in love a time before*

But it didn't work out right

This love for you I can't ignore

I try to run but I just can't hide… naw naw

Girl I put my trust in you

I'm not afraid of what my boys might say

Cause I know that my love is real

All I'm asking for is…"♫

Tears streamed down Micah's face as she watched Malik walk towards her dressed in all white just like she was. She was stunned that he had gone through so much to surprise her. Micah couldn't move as she saw cameras flashing.

♫*"A lifetime is all that I need*

I'm ready to settle down and give you all of me

I'm talking bout a lifetime

A lifetime is all that I need

Don't ever take your love away

I'll be here always..." ♬

By the time the chorus ended, Malik was down on one knee in front of Micah, holding a black box. When he opened it, Micah was nearly blinded. Oooh's and ahhh's could be heard throughout the room.

"A lifetime is all that I need baby... with you! Will you marry me?" Malik sincerely asked.

"YEESSS!!!! YES I'LL MARRY YOU!!" Micah screamed, as happy tears flowed freely down her beautiful face and with a big ass smile plastered on her face.

Malik stood up and slipped the ring onto her finger, and the crowd erupted in cheers.

"Oh my God... Malik, I can't believe you did all this. I love you so much!" Micah said as a fresh batch of tears streamed down her face.

"This is only the beginning baby! I love you too!" he told her and pulled her into his body and gave her a passionate kiss.

Micah began speaking to the guests after she cussed Candy out for tricking her and thanking her all in the same breath. Micah was so happy to see her parents there, especially her mom. The only person missing was Mark, but even if he had come home, Micah knew that he couldn't be out in a setting like that one yet.

"Congratulations Micah! I know we done bumped heads a lot, but I love you like a sister for real. You make my boy happy, and I'm happy for y'all. I just want you to know though, I didn't rape your bitch ass friend. She really ain't your friend, but it ain't my place to tell you. I hope you don't get caught up in any of her shit, because karma gon' catch her ass," Goo stated.

"Thank you Goo… I appreciate that. Let's let bygones be bygones… and you're right about Tasha. It took a lot for me to see, but I can clearly see that she ain't for me," Micah replied and gave Goo a hug.

"Awww… group picture. Come on Malik!" Candy called out, and he joined them instantly.

The cameraman took a picture of the four of them smiling from ear to ear.

"Candy, you really did all of this by yourself?" Micah questioned.

"I did… and it was sooo much fun," Candy beamed.

"Girl, you got mad skills," Micah complimented her.

"Thanks… I might start doing this on the side," Candy confessed.

Malik and Goo had walked off towards the front, and Micah and Candy made their way back towards the front as well.

"Are we done with pictures? It's bout time to come outta these heels," Micah affirmed.

"You can make it. Stay fly girl, it's your night," Candy chuckled.

Micah let Candy hype her up, so she didn't change into the flats that she had left in the car.

"Let's go do a toast on Snap Chat with the guys," Micah said as she pulled Candy with her.

As soon as she made it by the door, it opened, and an unknown woman walked in with a little boy. Micah had never seen her before and wondered if she was lost.

"Excuse me? Can I help you?" Micah asked her.

"Uhhh, I don't think so, but Malik can," the woman voiced.

"And just who the hell are you and how can my fiancé help you?" Micah asked with sass as she saw Malik staring at her out of the corner of her eye.

"I'm Nina... and this is MJ... his son!" the lady articulated.

"WHAT THE FUCK?" Micah hollered, grabbing not only Malik's attention, but everyone's in attendance as well.

***

Not believing his eyes, Malik kept his focus on the surreal scene that was unfolding right in front of him as he hurriedly made his way towards them. What the fuck was Nina doing at his engagement party? And who in the hell invited her? How the hell did she know where to find him after all this time? Were questions that were running through Malik's mind. She was the last motherfucking person that he expected to see tonight. Malik wanted to offer Micah some words to comfort her or to answer the many questions brought on by this very unwelcomed surprise; but hell, he was stumped himself. One thing was for sure, he was not about to let Nina come in and wreck the best thing that ever happened to him. That was for damn sure!

"Nina, what the fuck are you doing here?" Malik yelled, after finally making it to them.

"Hello to you too Malik. Looks like I'm right on time for the celebration. I brought MJ here to help you, or y'all rather, celebrate whatever it is that you're celebrating," Nina replied nonchalantly.

"What the hell you talkin' about Nina? You come to me after all this time playin' games? I'm not gonna ask yo ass again. WHY ARE YOU HERE? WHO THE FUCK IS MJ?" Malik challenged.

"I already told you that we're here for the celebration. Oh yeah, here's another tidbit that serves as a good reason to add to your celebration…your son. MJ is your son," Nina boasted blissfully to Malik and gave a gleeful smirk and a "now what bitch" look towards Micah, as she folded her arms across her chest and shifted all of her weight to her right leg.

Chapter 25

After the engagement party, Goo headed back to his crib. He planned on grabbing some clothes and heading back to Candy's place. He had been staying there with her for the past three weeks. He still hadn't heard from Mona, but she had been on his mind heavy lately. Not so much her, but the baby she was carrying that belonged to him. Goo pulled out his phone and hooked it up to the aux cord. He pulled up the Tidal app and went to Jay' Z latest album 4:44 and cruised the crazy streets in Chicago. Shawn Carter must have had him in a zone because he pulled up in front of the crib, quicker than he thought.

Goo killed the engine and hopped out. He pulled his keys from his pocket and placed them in the lock, granting him access. The house was pitch black. Goo walked directly to the living room and flicked on the light switch that was located to his right. When the lights flicked on, Goo's blood immediately began to boil when he saw the sight in front of him. The white French furniture that accompanied his all-white living room was ripped and torn into shreds. The 72 inch TV that was once mounted on the wall was lying face up with the screen smashed in. Someone took black and red spray paint and marked up everything, from the white African vases to the white Persian rugs. Pissed off to the max, Goo headed upstairs with hopes that they kept their vandalizing asses downstairs, but that hope quickly faded away when he hit his bedroom. The sheets were ripped off the bed and all of his clothes were pulled from his closet. The aroma of bleach filled the air as well as his clothes. Goo shook his head and chuckled lightly to himself. This shit was valueless and whoever did it only wasted their time. All of the material items could be replaced in a matter of minutes, but it was too bad the same couldn't be said about the culprit's life.

Goo headed back downstairs and right out the door. There was no need to grab clothes like he had originally planned since all his shit was fucked up. Goo knew niggaz didn't pull stunts such as the one pulled at his crib, that shit had "bitter bitch" written all over it. He thought about calling Mona, but for what? She wasn't going to answer and even if she did, he knew she wasn't going to confess to the shit. Goo said fuck it and turned his music up and rode off. He planned on staying with Candy until he hollered at his realtor Monday morning. A part of him was happy that Mona wasn't fucking with him while the other part knew this was just the beginning to some new bullshit.

"Got one baby mama, no bitch, no wife

Like Pac, ya need a thug in your life (yea...)

A young nigga to straight come through and beat it up

Let yo man be the freak, he can eat it up (ha haa)

Shorty got that fire she ain't let me down yet (nope)

Got that Aquafina flow

Call it wet wet"

Goo allowed Young Jeezy's lyrics from his first album "Thug Motivation 101" to serenade his ears as he hopped on the expressway. He took the Dan Ryan straight to 290. It was a little bit after one in the morning, so the streets were fairly clear. Flashbacks of the way his house looked replayed over and over in his head, and to be honest, the more and more he thought about it, it fucked with him. Goo snatched his phone from the cup holder and dialed Mona's number, and after about five rings, it went to voicemail.

"Bitch ass!" Goo said aloud to himself as he placed the phone back down.

As soon as the music started back up, it was interrupted by his ringing phone. Goo glanced down at it and was shocked to see Mona's name and picture flashing across the screen. Without an ounce of hesitation in his bones, he grabbed the phone, slid the bar across, and connected it to his car.

"MONA!" he raised his voice.

"RICO!" she yelled back.

"Are you out your motherfucking mind?" he asked and then paused to allow her time to speak, but instead she remained silent.

"Why the fuck you do the house like that? Imma choke the shit outta you, where you at?" he continued after she never said a word.

Mona let out an evil giggle before she finally addressed him.

"First of all, you ain't gon' do shit. Secondly, I do what the fuck I wanna do. Anymore questions?" she fired back.

Goo laughed to himself because she knew how to push all the wrong buttons, but he had to stay cool because he knew that Mona fed off shit like that.

"Look man, where the fuck you at?" he asked again.

"Why? Why? Why? Whhyyyyyyy?" Mona toyed with him, but Goo didn't let it faze him.

"Mona, where you at? I'm finna slide on you," he replied, trying his best to remain calm.

"Naw big fella, you ain't gon' make it to me," she laughed.

"Look, I know you mad, hurt, and upset or whatever, and you have every right to be; but you are still carrying my child. That's something you can never change," he reasoned with her.

The phone was silent for about seven seconds before Mona burst out in laughter and that shit was the final straw for Goo.

"KEEP FUCKN PLAYING WITH ME, IMMA…."

"You gon' what? You gon' kill me Rico? Kill me like you killed all those other people in your lifetime. Bitch, I ain't scared of you no more. You see, I tried to make this work, but you couldn't keep that little ass dick in your pants," she said, cutting him off.

Goo had to admit, the way Mona was speaking to him came as a shock. Being with her since they were teens, she always got mad, but that was the first time she got disrespectful.

"Look, I just wanna make sure you and the baby good," he lied. The truth was, he just needed to get her alone.

"Baby this and baby that. Nigga byyyeeeee! Only baby you care about is that big head ass little boy that belongs to Candy," Mona laughed like she was in the crowd of a Kevin Hart comedy show.

Goo's patience was wearing thin. He gritted his teeth before he spoke again.

"Man look, I love both of my kids, cut that shit out," he ordered, while he exited the expressway at Austin.

"BOTH KIDS? Nigga, how many you got?" she challenged.

That question completely caught Goo off guard.

"The fuck you mean?" he asked.

"Awwww… you mean the baby that I'm carrying? Silly…. Silly… silly Goo, this baby don't belong to you? Come on now! You really thought I was just chilling at the crib being dumb while you were out having fun? Boy, you gotta be smoking dope," she laughed uncontrollably.

Goo felt flames coming from his head as those words pierced his ears. He knew Mona was mad, but not to the point where she would confess anything.

"Mona, Imma fuck you up. Stop playing with me!" he yelled.

"Boy, ain't nobody playing, but I gotta go," Mona chuckled.

"Go where? We not done talking," he snapped.

"Oh, but we are done talking. As a matter of fact, I'll write you," she stated.

"Write me…. The fuck you mean write me?" Goo questioned.

The exact moment those words left his mouth, police sirens echoed through his ear. He sat up straight to look out the rearview mirror, blue and white lights flashed behind him. Without thinking twice, Goo pulled over.

"Mona. Mona. Mona," Goo called out while two police officers, both with their guns drawn, made their way to his car.

"Fuck you Goo. Don't drop the soap my nigga," was the last words he heard before Young Jeezy blasted through the speakers again, notifying him that she ended the call.

Chapter 26

Mona hung up the phone and smirked at her friend that was sitting in the passenger seat of her car. She knew that when it was all said and done, she would get the last laugh. Goo thought that he could do whatever the fuck he wanted to do, and she was supposed to lay down and take it, but he was sadly mistaken. Ever since that little sit down they had, where he left Mona high and dry, she began plotting. Although money wasn't a thing to Goo, it just felt good to destroy the shit that he had spent so much money on. Thoughts of burning the bitch down had crossed Mona's mind, but she dismissed them because she didn't want to bring any unnecessary attention on herself.

"Girl... you better not tell Goo I helped yo ass... I don't need him lookin' for me," Tika said.

"Bitch, Goo ass bout to be locked away for a long ass time. Them bricks that was placed in his ride is gonna secure that deal," Mona assured her.

"I hope you're right, because if not, he gon' kill yo ass. Why you didn't tell him about all them abortions you had? I bet that woulda really made his ass blow a fuse. Had him thinking you miscarried all them other times," Tika laughed.

"It really don't even matter. That nigga played me to the left for his side bitch. I don't want no baby by Goo... my real baby daddy bout to take over these streets fa sho now," Mona boasted.

"I heard that shit!" Tika commented.

"I appreciate your help...I'll have that package for you bright and early in the morning. I gotta get to my baby now though," Mona beamed as she turned into her friend's driveway.

"As many times as you done helped me out, you know I got ya back. Let me know if the next nigga decide to act up... whoever he is, wit yo secretive ass," Tika pointed out.

"You'll know in due time boo… in due time," Mona conceded.

After Mona dropped Tika off, she smiled at how everything had worked out in her favor. Goo was about to be sentenced for twenty years, she had the house, cars, and most importantly, the money. Her new man was about that life just like Goo, so there wouldn't be a change in her lifestyle. If Mona wasn't pregnant, she would take a drink just to celebrate her success. She looked at the radio and noticed that it was almost two o'clock. Mona never told her baby that she was coming. She knew that he would be breaking her off with some bomb as head and dick as soon as she told him that the plan they had come up with worked out perfectly.

Mona felt her baby kick, and she smiled and took one hand off of the steering wheel and rubbed her protruding belly.

"You ready to see daddy too? We'll be there soon," she cooed.

Twenty minutes later, Mona pulled up to her destination and parked. A light was on, which wasn't out of the norm because her man was known to stay up for twenty-four hours at a time. Mona looked to her left and saw the car that he told her belonged to his sister and silently wondered when she was going to take her ass home. Instead of calling, Mona walked up to the front door and knocked. When she heard what appeared to be fussing and someone threatening to leave, she froze because the voice sounded familiar.

"I been doing all this shit for you, and now you telling me, I gotta leave because of the next bitch. I tell you what nigga… you ain't gotta put me out. I'll leave on my own," the voice yelled.

"Cut the shit… you know I'm tryna handle shit. This whole shit wit us started out one way, but turned into something else. But don't get it twisted, I'll still break yo fuckin' neck," she heard him tell the unknown female.

Mona became pissed off because she didn't leave one fucked up situation to hop right into the next one. She twisted the door knob, and to her surprise, it was unlocked. Without thinking any further, Mona walked in and bumped right into the female who she heard screaming at her man.

"This bitch… you fuckin with this bitch?" Mona screamed.

"Yeah, he fuckin' wit this bitch just like ya husband was," Tasha spat.

Mona charged at her, but her man intervened.

"Chill out before you hurt my baby!" he demanded.

While he was holding her, Mona saw Tasha run out of the door at the speed of lightening all while talking shit. Her man broke loose from her and tried to chase Tasha, but he tripped. He walked over to the couch and felt under the cushion, but came up empty handed.

"That bitch took my gun!" Bear fumed.

"Why you fuckin' wit Tasha anyway? I didn't sign up for this shit!" Mona bickered.

"Because she my inside connect to finding out more information about the nigga that killed my team and tried to kill me," Bear spat!

To Be Continued…

Contest Time!!!

Answer these five questions and email your answers to
colehartreadersclub@gmail.com

To be fair and make sure you have followed the series thus far, 2 questions will be from book one and 3 questions are from book two. Contest ends Monday, 9-25-17 at 5:00 pm central time. The winner will be announced live in Twyla T's Reading Group and the winner will be emailed as well. Best wishes!!!

1. **What is M.O.M.??**
2. **Where does Micah attend college?**
3. **What are the name of the condos Malik bought Micah?**
4. **Who raped Tasha?**
5. **Who helped Mona destroy Goo's house and clothes?**

Sneak Peek

Pretty Lips That Thugs Love

By: Twyla T.

Chapter One

"Are you sure you wanna do this girl? I mean it's like murder ain't it?" Kya questioned her home girl Ashanti as she made the exit on Jack Warner Parkway in Tuscaloosa.

Ashanti really didn't want to have this conversation. She pondered over this pregnancy for a while now and she decided to do what was best for her.

Letting out a loud sigh, she said "Kya, you know Tay ain't bout to settle down and take care of no baby. Shit, I'll be stuck by my damn self and will be having to raise a kid alone. Besides, I'm almost four months pregnant so it's now or never and I pick now," Ashanti firmly stated.

Kya understood where her friend was coming from because she knew that Ashanti was speaking the truth about Tay.

"Aight... I feel you, but I hope Kentay's ass don't find out about this because I ain't got time for his bullshit, so we better hurry up," Kya replied while she was turning into the Women's Center. "Where's Raven at anyway? I thought she was bringing you," Kya continued while finding a place to park.

"She backed out since she's pregnant. Said she didn't feel right bringing me. I understand why," Ashanti replied as she nodded her head towards the parking lot. They looked at the protestors lined up marching and holding signs. Kya looked like she wanted to say something but kept her mouth closed. Looking at the protestors for another second, Ashanti turned her head away from the window and concentrated back on the task at hand. Ashanti didn't give a fuck about the protestors because she saw them the week before when she had her first appointment. Why she had to go through two appointments was still crazy to her, she inwardly thought. However, she reminded herself that she had to do what she had to do because Tuscaloosa was closer than Memphis.

Ashanti was having second thoughts about going through the with procedure and just keeping her baby because she didn't really want to go through an abortion, but she knew having a baby at the moment just wasn't in the plans. Ashanti knew that Kentay wouldn't do right no matter how many promises he made and even though she was going to school less than an hour away from home, she would make the best of her scholarship at Mississippi State University. Scoring a 25 on her ACT allowed her to pick pretty much any school she wanted, but Ashanti always wanted to attend State. It was sentimental to her since her dad graduated from there, and he died when she was ten.

Before they could get out of the car, Kya's little white Honda Civic started shaking as a reaction from the booming sound system of a truck that had pulled up right behind them. The way the truck was angled, it was clear that the owner was making sure they couldn't get away. The windows were tinted so black, even the back one which was facing Ashanti, that you couldn't see who was inside. She did notice that there were no tags on it yet, and she silently prayed Tay hadn't went and bought a new vehicle. Ashanti stared at the candy red Hummer sitting on 26's and a lump formed in her throat and her heart starting pounding hard in her chest when her boyfriend Kentay prepared to exit the vehicle. Both Ashanti and Kya were shocked and in total disbelief to see Tay walking towards their vehicle.

"Fuck! That prayer didn't get answered. How did he know where I was?" Ashanti spewed through gritted teeth to her girl who had just gotten out of the driver seat. Kya shrugged and ignored the question as she exited her car. She discreetly turned her camera on record mode because she knew some shit was about to pop off that would be worth capturing.

Kentay walked slowly towards Ashanti with *Trap Queen* by Fetty Wap blasting through the sound system. The expression on his face let her know that he was pissed the fuck off. Trying to buy herself some time and distance from him, Ashanti frantically began talking.

"What are you doing here? How did you find me? How did you know I was pregnant?" she asked, not giving him a chance to answer the first question. She noticed that he wasn't trying to answer her questions, so Ashanti tried to turn and walk the other way. However, she was too slow and didn't get away quick enough. Kentay didn't give one fuck about where he was and what he was about to do. Before Ashanti knew it, he snatched her up and threw her against the car and began choking her.

"I know good and got damn well you ain't bout to kill my mu'fuckin baby!" he spat as his grip became tighter and tighter around her neck. Ashanti couldn't answer even if she wanted to because his grip was so strong. The only thing she could do was claw at him and tried to pry his hands from cutting off her passage of air. The more she fought, the tighter his grip became so she finally succumbed to his wrath. After realizing that she had stopped struggling, Tay let her and Ashanti dropped to the ground in a coughing fit. Ashanti rubbed her neck while still coughing, trying her best to ease the pain. She knew there would be marks on her bronze color skin because she bruised easily.

Kentay stared down at her trying to calm himself and to get control of his emotions. Meanwhile, Kya recorded everything from the opposite side of the car while his homeboy, Slick, sat in the passenger seat of his truck smoking on some Kush and talking on the phone. Having witness these types of shenanigans between Kentay and Ashanti before, Slick shook his head at his friend and continued his conversation. For that reason alone, Slick knew exactly what was going on but dared not to intervene because it wasn't his business.

Moments later, Ashanti got her breathing back under control but remained sitting on the ground. When Ashanti looked up, she stared at the man that she loved with her whole heart as he towered down over her with his six-foot frame. As pissed off as she was, she couldn't help but to stare at everything that she fell in love with about him. His muscular frame turned her on from the jump, along with his dark brown bedroom eyes and smooth golden skin. Kentay was a ladies' man no doubt, but Ashanti couldn't resist his charm. He always wore a serious expression on his face, and people knew not to fuck with him. Shaking and trembling from the inside out, Ashanti was scared to death because it was the first time she had been on the receiving end of his wrath in that manner. She wasn't sure of what he would do next, so she decided to just stay still.

After what seemed like an eternity, Kentay bent down and pulled Ashanti up roughly.

"If you ever try to do some shit like this again, I'll kill yo ass. You know I love you, and I'ma always hold you down so stop tripping and shit. Now give me a kiss with them big, juicy ass lips," he said, speaking to her as if she was a child and pulled Ashanti's body closer to him and gripped her thick hips and fat ass. Ashanti didn't know how to respond, so she just remained quiet. Tay had her five foot five inch framed pulled close to him so he couldn't see the tears that were threatening to fall.

After a few moments, Tay finally noticed the fear in her eyes, and he tried to soothe her as best he could.

"I'm sorry baby, but you know how I get when you act crazy," Tay told her and kissed those luscious lips that he loved so much. Ashanti yielded to him without putting up much of a fuss. He rubbed his hands all over her body, giving her ass and hips extra attention like they were at home instead of outside in the parking lot of a Women's Clinic. For some reason, Shanti just couldn't shake Tay. It was probably because he was all that she knew.

"Yo Slick, hop in with Kya while my baby get in wit me," Kentay said to his homeboy. Slick nodded his head in understandment and made the move to switch vehicles. Tay ushered Ashanti to the passenger side and helped her to get in the truck. As Ashanti put her seatbelt on, Kya walked over to the truck, and Ashanti rolled the window down.

"Call me later boo," Kya said with much concern and gave Ashanti her iPhone and purse that she had dropped on the ground. Unable to speak, Ashanti gave Kya a nod, took her stuff and placed them in her lap.

Kentay pulled out of the parking lot and starting riding with both of them deep into their own thoughts. With her head resting on the seat and eyes closed, Ashanti prayed that having this baby would make Tay do right by her, but deep down she felt like it was only going to add to their problems.

"I can't believe you was bout to kill my seed ma. I expect that type of shit from these hoes out in the streets, but not you," Kentay said in a tone filled with shock and disgust, finally breaking the silence after riding for about fifteen minutes.

"Tay, it's not like our relationship is perfect," Ashanti replied after a few more moments of silence.

"Ain't no relationship perfect, but communication is everything. Don't ever do no shit like this again. I got you, and I got my lil man no matter what," he told her and reached over and rubbed her stomach.

"How you know it's a boy?" Ashanti asked while smiling.

"I just know," Kentay answered and smirked.

Silence filled the truck once more. It wasn't until then that Ashanti noticed that they weren't headed back towards home; instead, they were on Interstate 20 going east. Taking a peak in her direction, he could see confusion written all over her.

"Just sit tight. I got you," Tay said and kept driving. Before she knew it, Ashanti had dosed off. When she woke up, Tay was turning off of 459. Looking in Tay's direction, she smiled and started feeling excited because she'd figured out where they were heading. Ashanti knew he was going to the restaurant she mentioned to him the last time they rode through Birmingham. Ashanti loved Italian food and mentioned Gianmarco's Restaurant to Tay because of the great reviews. That was about six months ago, and she had forgotten about it. Evidently he hadn't.

They walked in and were seated within five minutes. It was fifteen minutes after eleven, so they beat the lunch hour crowd and placed their orders right away. When the waitress walked away, Kentay pulled a box out of his pocket. Ashanti's hands went straight over her mouth.

"Oh my gawwddd!!" Ashanti squeaked when he opened the box and laid eyes on the platinum diamond ring.

"Wait a minute… calm down baby!" Kentay said trying to keep her from jumping the gun. "This ain't no engagement ring. It's a friendship ring. I'm only twenty-three and you eighteen so ain't neither one of us ready for marriage, but as long as you wearing this ring, I got you," he told her. Tears were forming in Ashanti's eyes.

"It's beautiful baby," she finally said. "I just want you to stay committed to me," Ashanti continued.

"I got you baby. I'm working on getting better for you," Kentay replied.

"I hope so baby, but don't do it for me. Do it for you. I can't keep going back and forth with all of these thots tryna prove my love when I shouldn't have to," Ashanti retorted.

"I know. You've been holding me down for almost three years, and I appreciate you. This is my way of moving in the right direction. It ain't gon happen overnight, but we gon get there. I love you girl," Tay sincerely replied. He knew that Ashanti had to do a lot of sneaking and going against what her mother said to be with him, so he told himself that it was time to step up and do right by her.

Ashanti finally noticed two keys hanging from the ring after picking it up and out of the box, and was shocked.

"What are the keys for?" she inquired.

"When we leave here, I'ma show you," he told her.

After finishing their delicious meals, Kentay paid the bill and they left. Ashanti wasted no time posting her ring on every social media site she had an account for as soon as she got settled in the truck. Her notifications were blowing up on Facebook, Snap Chat, Instagram, and Twitter. She captioned the picture with the hashtags #HisForever #ImWifey #PleaseBelieveIt and also took an off guard picture of him driving and tagged him on Facebook. Kentay barely got on Facebook, but Ashanti tagged him in pictures so the hoes would know she wasn't going anywhere. The crazy thing about their relationship is that she never caught him cheating. However, there was always a different female calling and texting Ashanti about Tay, so she knew for them to be that bold, something had to be going on no matter how much he denied it.

Two hours later, Kentay lightly shook Ashanti after he parked. Ashanti didn't even realize she had gone to sleep. When she focused, she wondered what in the world they were doing at Carpenter Place. They were parked at the new condos on Louisville Street in Starkville.

"What are we doing here?" Shanti inquired.

"Get out and let's see. Be sure you grab those keys," he told her. Ashanti got out behind Kentay and followed him. They were parked in front of building G, which was in the back, and Kentay stopped at door number four. Ashanti put one of the keys in the lock and it opened. When she walked inside, her mouth hit the floor. The place looked like it came straight off of HGTV. The wooden floors were glistening and the living area was very spacious. Ashanti could see the beautiful marble top on the island and fell in love with it instantly. An 80-inch flat screen was mounted on the wall with a sound bar connected to it. Ashanti walked slowly through the place not believing it could get any better, but she was wrong. She walked into the master bedroom and slipped off her shoes because the carpet was so pretty and white. It felt like cotton in between her toes. There was a California King bed in the center of the floor, and it was already decorated in red and black. The bathroom had a walk in shower, a Jacuzzi, his and her sinks and it was color coordinated with the décor from the bedroom.

Realizing she hadn't said a word since she entered the apartment, she turned towards Kentay.

"Baby is this our place?" Ashanti finally asked after doing a complete walk through of the entire condo.

"It's yours. Everything here is in your name. Of course I'll be here, but it's all yours baby. I know you going to school here, so you need to be close to campus instead of driving back and forth," he smiled and told her.

Not sure of what to say, Ashanti said the first thing that came to her mind.

"Well you know my motor went out in my car so I was gonna stay on campus anyway," she responded with total surprise still lacing her voice.

"I got that taken care of too," Kentay said proudly and pulled a key out of his pocket and handed it to her.

"You bought me a car too?" Ashanti excitedly questioned. "Where is it?" she asked and started walking towards the front.

"Hit the alarm," Tay replied. Ashanti quickly opened the door and looked out to see which vehicle the key belonged to.

BEEP! BEEP!

She did as he said and the alarm beeped to a brand new red 2016 Range Rover.

"Oh my gawwddd!! You bought me a Range," Ashanti screamed and ran and hopped in. Her name was engraved in the steering wheel as well as the custom made floor mats. She checked out all of the features while Kentay stood there smiling at her. "Baby, I can't believe you did all of this for me. Thank you so much," Ashanti cried and tears started streaming down her face.

"You're welcome baby girl. It's the least I can do. I give different kids scholarships for college all the time, so what I look like not making sure my girl and my baby are taken care of?" Tay replied. Ashanti got out of the truck and kissed him sensually.

After kissing for what seemed like forever, Kentay pulled his lips from Ashanti, trying to get some much needed air.

"Damn, you got my dick hard as fuck. You bout to throw me off track. I gotta go and take care of some business, but you keep my pussy wet for me. I'll be back later," Tay told her and kissed her again and squeezed her ass before hopping in his Hummer and leaving. Ashanti was smiling from ear to ear when she went back in and walked around her new place. "I knew he loved me. Things are starting to look up thanks to you," she cooed to the baby while rubbing her stomach.

Chapter Two

After putting a smile on Ashanti's face, Tay headed out to Black Jack to take care of some business. Kentay was the man in the Golden Triangle area. As much as he tried not to be flashy, he just couldn't help himself. He was proud of the name he built for himself over the years. Ten years ago, at the tender age of thirteen, Tay started running the streets. He caught his first body six short months after that. Nino, the old head he was running for, took care of everything and instilled in him ways to never get caught. Since the relationship Tay had with his dad was pretty much nonexistent, he looked up to Nino, and in return, Nino treated him like the son he never had. When Nino died five years ago, his entire empire fell into the hands of eighteen year old Kentay Mills. Since he had been properly groomed, the transition was sweet. Many hated on him, but he didn't have one fuck to give. All he wanted to do was make money and help people, whether it was putting them on to work or through scholarships and other services he provided throughout the community and state.

Many looked at Kentay as a hypocrite because the same shit that he was selling was what took his mom out years ago. He remembered May 10, 2005 like it was yesterday.

It was a hot and humid day when Kentay and Slick left school Thursday afternoon, but it didn't keep them from going to their favorite spot on the West Side to shoot basketball. They walked from school up on Henderson Hill and went straight to the court. Both of them loved the game and had plans on trying out for the middle school basketball team at Armstrong the next year. Slick had his basketball, dribbling between his legs and Tay went in for the steal and succeeded. He took the ball and ran to the court and dunked it.

"You better tighten up or I'ma rip you every time man," Tay said to his boy semi-bragging, but also schooling him. They ended up playing one on one until the crowd showed up, and then the full court games began.

Kentay and Slick always played on the same team and everyone knew it, but that never stopped the hating. They had become immune to it and didn't entertain it because Slick's mom was strict on him and would make him come straight home if he got into any kind of trouble. Kentay on the other hand, his mom never forced him to be home at a certain time. Out of respect for his friend, he still tried to keep his anger in check and ignore the assholes to stay out of trouble because they always had each other's back.

The day went well on the court, like it pretty much always did. About six o'clock, Kentay started walking with Slick towards his house. Kentay lived in Brooksville Garden, which was known as The Garden around town. However, they bypassed it and headed towards Reed's Place, which was on down the road so that Slick could get home on time. Slick obeyed the rules as much as possible and tried not to argue with his mom because he didn't like to put extra stress on her. Although she never said it, she stressed every single day over his dad. Slick's nickname was given to him after his dad, who was serving a twenty-five year bid in prison for a string of crimes that consisted of carjacking, bank robberies, and breaking and entering. Not many knew what his real name was because he hated it, but even the ones who did called him Slick after his dad because he looked exactly like him. Suzanne, Slick's mom, hated that nickname, but there was nothing she could do to stop the name. She vowed to make sure her son stayed on the straight and narrow, which was why she was so strict.

When they made it to her house, she invited Kentay in for dinner, just like she always did. He sat down and ate chicken and rice with them before heading home.

"I'll see you tomorrow man," Kentay said to Slick after he finished eating and got up to leave. "Thanks for dinner Mrs. Hudson," he told Suzanne and gave her a hug before leaving. During the walk home, Tay made a pit stop by the store to grab some red Kool-Aid. He knew his mom probably wasn't home yet, so he wasn't in a hurry. It was almost nine o'clock by the time he made it home. Using his key, he went inside and an eerie feeling came over him. Brushing it off, he went straight to the kitchen to make the Kool-Aid. As soon as he started ripping the Kool-Aid packages open, Tay heard a loud noise coming from the back.

What the hell he thought to himself and went and grabbed the bat that was placed behind the front door before going to check things out. Walking quietly towards the back, Kentay gripped the bat tight, ready to bust someone's skull. He heard some faint moans coming from towards the bathroom and rushed in with the bat midair. When he saw who it was, he dropped the bat immediately and ran to his mother's side. Looking beside her on the floor, he knew exactly what was going on, but said a prayer that his mom would be okay. He turned the water on in the tub, took the shower head and started spraying cold water on her face. When she didn't move after several moments, he ran and called 911.

Less than fifteen minutes later, everyone was outside being nosey as paramedics rolled Kenya out of the house on the gurney covered with a white sheet. Mrs. Suzanne took Kentay in, but he just didn't want to live there forever. He turned to the streets a year later and never looked back. Slick was true to his boy and rode with him, disobeying his mother for the first time. The bond they shared was unbreakable.

The ringing of Kentay's phone broke him from his thoughts.

"What up?" he answered.

"You coming through?" the voice on the other end asked. He hesitated for a moment, but finally answered.

"Yeah, I'm on my way. We need to talk," he replied and hung up without waiting for a reply. He turned his music up and blasted *YFN* by Lucci while on his way to The Links.

It's either now or never
Right now I'm high as ever
One of the hottest ever
I'm just being modest
I'mma be the topic
They talk about forever
When they ask about me
Just make sure you tell em
We just some young fly niggas (Yeah)
We just some young fly niggas (Yeah)
We just some young fly niggas (Yeah)

Kentay pulled up to his destination thirty minutes later. For some strange reason, he was nervous, but he knew that he needed to get inside and handle his business. Before he could even knock, the door swung open, and he was greeted by a smiling face. She knew exactly what he liked, so she wasted no time unbuckling his pants and pushing him towards the sofa.

"Wait... wait," he started to say.

"Let me take care of you and then we can talk," she replied.

"What the hell," he told himself and laid back and got ready to enjoy the bomb ass head that he was about to receive. Kentay's dick was already standing at attention before he felt her tongue teasing his tip. Being a sucker for a woman with a fat ass who could give some fye head was one of his weaknesses, and the girl who sucking his dick like she taught Super head her skills knew just that.

"Ohhh shiiittt!" Kentay moaned while receiving some superb dome.

"You like that baby?" she asked him, knowing good and damn well he was enjoying every second of it. A few minutes later, Kentay felt his nut rising and tried to get up, but he was held in place and all of his future kids went straight down her throat. She swallowed them with a smile plastered on her face.

"Got damn girl!" he huffed and laid his head back. He knew she was ready to fuck, but he just couldn't do it. Sleeping with her had been a mistake that turned into mistake after mistake at least three times a week for the past few months. He blamed the very first time on his drunkenness. After that though, there was no excuse and he knew it, which was why he was about to end things once and for all.

After going to the bathroom to gather himself, Kentay walked back out ready to deliver the speech that he had rehearsed in his head over and over and over.

"Why you hop up so fast? You know if I coulda hopped on it, I would have," she told him.

"Listen, we gotta stop this. It's not cool, and I gotta take a stand. I didn't intend to come here and get my dick sucked, but it is what it is. I don't want anyone to get hurt, and if we keep this up that's exactly what is gonna happen so we gotta end this shit. It's foul on all levels, and I can't keep doing this to my girl. We bout to be a real family. I hope you understand, and I truly hope you feel the same way," Kentay said as nicely as he could.

"Your girl? You weren't thinking about your girl while ramming your dick in me these last few months. But for real though, why you wanna end something this good? Besides, I love you," she confessed.

"Ain't no way you love me. That's just lust because I been dicking you down with this anaconda, but we can't do it no mo. Real talk," he told her. When he noticed the tears welling up in her eyes, he tried to continue being nice, but knew he had to be firm. "Hey, you need to focus on your family. You got a baby on the way and a nice standup guy. Be the woman he needs you to be," Kentay pleaded and turned towards the door to leave. Not giving in so easily, she confessed something that she had been keeping close to her chest.

"But my baby is yours Tay," she sobbed and his hand froze on the doorknob.

Chapter Three

Ashanti couldn't contain her excitement after Tay left, so she decided she would fix a nice candlelight dinner to show her appreciation. When she went into the kitchen and looked in the cabinets and refrigerator, everything was fully stocked, and it made her smile that much more. Her massive walk-in closet in the master bedroom was already full of clothes, but she still needed to go to her mom's house in Weir and gather some of her favorite items. After pulling out a few items she needed to prepare dinner, Ashanti grabbed her cell phone and called her mom. She already knew how the conversation was going to go, but decided it was time to get it over with.

"Hey Shanti… are you on your way home? I need you to grab some Clorox for me," her mom Tina asked as soon as she answered after two rings.

"Hey mom! I wasn't planning on coming today, but if you need it today I can get Kya to drop it by there," Ashanti replied.

"You just don't spend no time at home. You already bout to go to college in a couple of months. I thought you would be home more after graduation, but let me guess, you with that thug," Tina stated.

"He's not a thug mom, but I was calling to give you some good news," Ashanti stated defending her baby's daddy.

"Hmph… I just call it like I see it. You been running behind that boy these past few years just going damn crazy," Mrs. McNeal said.

"Anyways mom… I got a new condo… and you're also about to be a grandma," Ashanti nervously said in a rushed tone. A silent pause met Ashanti on the other end of the line. Tina was so quiet that Ashanti had to pull her cell phone away from her ear to make sure that her mom hadn't hung up on her. "Did you hear me mom?" Ashanti asked after the line was silent for a few moments.

"I heard you. I'm just a bit shocked at the last statement. You know how hard it was for me having you at a young age. I just thought that you would make better choices than me. Did the thug try to make you have an abortion?" Tina revolted.

"No mom, he didn't. We are doing good right now. He got me my own place, and the lease is in my name. I wish you would come to Starkville and visit," Ashanti said, feeling hopeful.

"Well, I'll definitely be by there, but I wish you were staying in a dorm and getting the full college experience. But with a baby on the way, I guess you need your own space. How far along are you anyway?" her mom asked.

"Four months," Ashanti mumbled, but her mom heard her loud and clear.

"FOUR MONTHS?! Really Ashanti? FOUR MONTHS?" Mrs. McNeal screamed.

"I know mom… I didn't want to tell you like this, but I didn't want you to find out from anyone else. I'm about to cook so I'll call you later," Ashanti said and rushed off of the phone to prevent hearing further disappointment in her mom's voice.

While the steaks were cooking, Ashanti whipped up some loaded mashed potatoes and asparagus. Since they had eaten Italian food earlier, she decided this would be the perfect meal to break in her new place. Figuring she could pass a little time, Ashanti grabbed her phone and logged onto Snap Chat and started viewing stories. When she noticed clips of the incident from earlier with Tay, she became pissed off and called Kya right away.

"Bitch, why the fuck you post that shit on Snap Chat?" Shanti spat as soon as her girl answered the phone.

"Bitch, we always play bout shit like that. Why you mad now?" Kya asked, surprised that Ashanti sounded angry and would call her about the video.

"That nigga choked me up so what was even funny about that? Yeah we post crazy shit all the time but I didn't record or post shit when Ryan went upside your head," Ashanti fumed.

"I'll delete the shit. I wasn't being funny damn," Kya compromised.

"All your damn followers prolly done saw the shit bout now and shared it. Snap Chat messy asses let you share other people's stories without you even knowing now remember," Ashanti said while shaking her head.

"Damn, I forgot all about that. I wasn't thinking and it was just a joke. I figured you woulda saw it by now anyway. What you been doin?" Kya inquired trying to take the heat off of her ass.

Ashanti filled Kya in on everything that happened after they parted ways and told her that her that she was shocked she didn't see the pictures all over social media. Kya informed her that she logged off right after posting on Snap Chat and went to visit a friend. They talked a little more about meeting up the next day to finalize everything for Raven's baby shower that would occur in just a few days, and then they hung up. Ashanti heard the door slam just as she was taking the garlic bread out of the oven and smiled.

"Damn, it smells good in here," Kentay said walking into the kitchen.

"You're right on time baby," Ashanti bragged and kissed him when he pulled her in for a hug.

"I'ma go hop in the shower right quick. I'll be back," Tay told her. Before she could reply, her phone rang and she answered.

"Hello, what's up chic? You gon live a long time, I was just talking bout you girl," Ashanti greeted.

"Oh yeah? You and who? Your punk ass boyfriend?" Raven asked in an annoyed voice.

"Watch your mouth talking about my boo... but nah I was talking to Kya," Ashanti defensively replied. "You ready for Saturday?" she continued ignoring her friend's mood.

"Yes! I'm so excited. I still don't know why y'all wouldn't let me help with the planning," Raven whined.

"We got you girl... besides, you'll get to plan mine next," Ashanti excitedly stated.

"Oh my gawdd... What? You pregnant" Raven said as sarcastically as she could.

"Damn! You got jokes like you didn't know. What the hell is wrong wit you?" Ashanti asked slightly offended.

"Nothing girl, I was just joking don't act so uptight," Raven muffled while trying to reign in her emotions.

"Well... let me get done with dinner before Tay gets outta the shower," Ashanti responded still confused by her friend's reaction.

"That nigga probably been fucking someone else if he came in and got straight in the shower. You better check him," Raven confidently stated.

"Bye Raven," Ashanti snapped, becoming frustrated and hung up.

When Kentay walked back into the dining area, he immediately noticed that Ashanti's mood had slightly changed by the expression on her face.

"What's wrong babe?" he asked her.

"Nothing, let me fix our plates." Ashanti tried to ignore her emotions and got up from the table.

"Nah I got it. You cooked, so just relax and I'll fix em," Tay said and headed into the kitchen.

Ashanti sat back down and waited while Kentay fixed the plates. She pondered on whether or not she was going to address her feelings. Raven always said slick shit about Kentay and Ashanti didn't understand why.

"I know this bout to be good," Tay said as he sat Ashanti's plate in front of her and then sat his across from her and took his seat. "So what's wrong babe? We said we was gonna communicate better and shit. You was fine when I walked in and now you looking like you been sucking on lemons," Tay said after taking a couple of bites of food.

"Raven," Ashanti said barely audible and Kentay dropped his fork.

"What about her?" he asked after regaining his composure.

"She's always throwing shade and shit. Here I am planning her baby shower, and she talking about if you came home and hopped right in the shower, you was probably just out fucking another bitch," Ashanti stated.

"She's jealous. I still don't know why you deal with her, but I can't choose your friends for you," Kentay said trying to play off his growing anger.

"We've been friends forever. I know she had her ways, but I do love her and want her in my life. She's been there for me through some of my hardest times just like I have been for her," Shanti replied.

"Well, we not bout to let her mess up our night. The day started out shaky and shit, but it turned out for the best, so let's finish this bomb ass meal you cooked and then we can relax," Tay retorted.

"You're right baby. That's why I love you," Ashanti happily declared.

"I love you too girl," he told her and then dived back into his meal.

When they finished eating, Kentay led Ashanti to the master bathroom and started running water so that she could soak in the Jacuzzi. He slowly undressed her and admired her body and rubbed her stomach that had a small pudge.

"All this time, I thought you were just getting thicker, but you're carrying my son," he said and bent down and kissed her stomach. He assisted her with getting stepping in the Jacuzzi and then sat on the side and started rubbing her shoulders. Thinking about the event from that morning, Ashanti wanted to know the answers to her question.

So as she relaxed, she said "Babe, how did you know where I was this morning anyway?" Ashanti asked with her eyes closed while enjoying his strong hands massaging her shoulders.

"We just gon leave that in past baby," he replied with the best answer that he could think of. He didn't want to reveal his source as it would undoubtedly lead to more questions.

Ashanti dropped the subject because she wanted to keep the atmosphere pleasant. After Kentay finished massaging her and washing her off, he scooped her up and wrapped a towel around her body.

"The parts that the towel didn't dry, I'ma lick it off," he whispered to her and placed her in the middle of the California King. Ashanti shivered with pleasure as she looked into Tay's eyes because she knew what was about to happen and she couldn't wait. After Kentay slipped his clothes off, he climbed in the bed in his birthday suit and kissed Ashanti's pretty lips sweetly while his hands roamed all over her tender body. He began making a trail of kisses down her body, not missing one spot. When he reached her breasts, he gave both of them the same amount of attention before moving further south.

When Kentay reached Shanti's wet mound, he inserted two fingers before nibbling on her clit, causing her juices to flow instantly. One of the things that she loved about Kentay was he always knew exactly what she needed. There were times when she wanted to be made love to like he was doing at the moment, and then there were times when she wanted to be fucked. She would get that the next morning. Getting lost in her thoughts, Ashanti felt Tay's rock hard dick easing into her tightness. She gasped as he entered. They had fucked and made love countless of times, but it still always took a few moments for her to get used to his ten inches penetrating her every single time.

After he stroked her slowly a few times, Ashanti started rotating her hips and matching Kentay thrust for thrust.

"Umm… shit! You feel so good baby," Ashanti moaned while pulling Tay closer to her.

"Not as good as you. You bet not ever give my pussy away! You hear me?" Tay demanded while deep stroking her.

"I… I… won't baby!" Ashanti stuttered.

"Whose pussy is this?" he asked while pounding her.

"It's yours… all yours daddy!" Shanti said while digging her nails into his back.

"It better be. Now flip that ass over and back it up on this dick," Tay told her and she happily obliged.

Ashanti knew that Tay loved hitting it from the back, but she also knew that he wouldn't last long with her throwing it back at him. She twerked on his dick and then creamed all over it before he shot what seemed like a pound of cum in her.

"Got damn… if you wasn't already pregnant you damn shol woulda got pregnant off of that," Tay chuckled and collapsed beside her on the bed. They both laughed as they cuddled. "You need to make an appointment and let me know when it is. We gotta make sure our son is Gucci," Tay said while rubbing her stomach.

"I'll call first thing in the morning," Shanti sleepily replied.

"Cool… now get some rest because I'm tired as fuck," Tay said, then closed his eyes. Ashanti smiled and was happy about the turn of events in her life. She silently thanked God and snuggled closer to Kentay and then drifted off to sleep.

CPSIA information can be obtained
at www.ICGtesting.com
Printed in the USA
LVHW041156291119
638735LV00023B/949/P

9 781979 111515